Virginia Vineyards

LOVE CHILD

USA TODAY BESTSELLING AUTHOR

ASHLEY FARLEY

CHAPTER 1

C asey sees the last of the movers to the door and turns to face the empty apartment, her home for most of her twenty-six years. Soft gray walls. Worn random-width oak floors. Windows overlooking Central Park. The furnishings are gone—the priceless antiques and extensive art collection sold to an auction house to help pay medical bills. And her mother's wardrobe and personal effects all donated to charity. While Casey hated to give her mother's belongings away, she has no place to keep them and no money to splurge on a storage unit.

Sliding down to the hardwood floor, she rests her head against the wall and closes her eyes. She can almost hear her mother singing loud and off key down the hall in the cramped corner kitchen—selections from classic musicals like *West Side Story* and *Oklahoma*. Her mother couldn't hold a tune, but she sure could cook. Several times a month, Beverly invited her famous friends over for dinner. She hired waitstaff to serve and clean up, but she insisted on preparing the meal herself.

Tears stream down Casey's cheek. She'll never again hear her mother sing, never taste her gourmet cooking. Memories and a handwritten letter are all she has left of Beverly Hobbs, glamorous anchor of a nationally syndicated morning news show.

Casey tugs the crumpled paper free of her back pocket. Her mother had left instructions for her attorney to give the letter to Casey upon her death. For as long as she can remember, Casey had hounded her mother for information about her father. Where does he live? How does he earn his living? Do I look like him? Her mother's answers were vague. They'd met when Beverly was in California on a business trip. They had a drunken one-night stand, and Beverly remembered little about him, including his name.

But her mother's letter tells a different tale, the story of the summer she spent with Daniel Love in Napa. Beverly was taking a much-needed break from her demanding job at the network, and Daniel, a vintner from Virginia, was conducting research on the winemaking process. At the end of the summer, their affair ended, and Daniel returned to his wife and family—the wife and family he'd failed to mention until their last night together. Beverly was heartbroken. She would never find another love like the one they'd shared. When she discovered she was pregnant two months later, she viewed the baby as a gift from God, her love child.

Wiping away the tears, Casey gets to her feet and goes to the window, staring down at the new green foliage on the trees in Central Park. For the past three years, she's watched the seasons change from the room down the hall while nursing her mother. Casey had been making a name for herself as a graphic designer when she quit her job to take care of Beverly. Three of the most critical career-building years of her life wasted. She has nothing to show for that time except a meager sum in her bank account, two suitcases of shabby clothes, and her mother's 2005 baby blue Volvo convertible. Her friends have moved on with their lives. No reputable graphics firm in New York will hire her. Her future is a blank slate. And Virginia is calling her name. What if things don't work out with her father? She'll worry about that if it happens.

Turning her back on the window, she grabs her suitcases and

leaves the apartment. She retrieves the convertible from the garage and navigates the city streets to open roads.

Casey's mind drifts as she imagines the reunion with her father. She has the advantage. She knows who he is. He's unaware she's alive. She envisions herself bursting in on a Love family dinner—her father's shock, his wife's outrage, and their children's confusion when she announces her identity. Casey chuckles to herself. She's mild-mannered by nature. She could never do something so bold.

Casey had considered searching the Internet for information about the man, his family, and their vineyard. Fearing she might discover something that would dissuade her from making the trip, she decides to go in blind.

Casey spends the night at a roadside motel near Richmond and drives into the Virginia mountains the following morning. The town of Lovely is smaller than she'd imagined, but way more charming with upscale boutiques and restaurants lining Magnolia Avenue, the primary thoroughfare. She'd skipped breakfast, and even though it's not yet noon, her stomach is rumbling for lunch. She parks in front of Ruthie's Diner and enters the restaurant. Only a handful of patrons occupy red upholstered stools at the lunch counter, leaving Casey her choice of tables. She chooses a two-top by the window.

An attractive middle-aged woman, her white-blonde hair piled high on her head, slides a laminated menu in front of her. "Our specials today are white bean chili and turkey reuben. Can I offer you something to drink? I just made a fresh pot of coffee. Or, if you prefer something refreshing, our sweet tea is famous around these parts, not too sweet with the right amount of freshly squeezed lemon."

Casey's eyes travel the woman's curvaceous figure, landing on the name tag pinned to her ample breast. "Ruthie? So, you're the owner?"

Ruthie's bubblegum-pink lips part in a smile. "I am. What brings you to town? Or are you just passing through?"

Unexpected tears fill Casey's eyes. "I'm . . ." Her voice cracks, preventing her from saying more.

Ruthie bends over to get a better look at her. "Are you all right, hon?"

Casey breathes in an unsteady breath. "Not really. I just lost my mother. I'm from New York, and I needed a change of scenery."

"I'm sorry to hear that, sweetheart. But you came to the right place. The fresh mountain air will do you good."

"Can you recommend an affordable hotel?"

"There's only one choice." Ruthie inclines her head at the building across the street. "The Red Robin Inn, although I wouldn't classify it as affordable. They're booked most weekends, but since today is Tuesday, I'm sure they have availability. You might even get a discounted rate. The courtyard rooms are smaller and less expensive."

"Great. I'll check it out."

Ruthie shifts her weight. "Why did you pick Lovely? Do you have family in town?"

Casey pretends not to hear her. "I'll have sweet tea and . . ." She scans the menu, ordering the first thing that catches her eye—the arugula salad with goat cheese, fresh berries, and grilled chicken.

"Coming right up," Ruthie says, scribbling on her notepad as she walks away.

Casey mulls over her dilemma while she waits for her food. She can't afford an extended stay at a pricey hotel. But she doesn't want to blindside her father. The slow approach will better serve everyone involved. Besides, she's in no hurry. She has nowhere else to be. The blank canvas is stretched on the frame, waiting for Casey to paint the first stroke of her new life.

When Ruthie returns with her tea, Casey says, "This is a cute town. I may decide to stay. Any chance you're hiring?"

"No, unfortunately." Ruthie sweeps a hand at the empty tables. "Business is slow Monday through Wednesday. While we make up for it on the weekends, I have to give my staff as many hours as possible."

Casey's smile fades. "I understand."

"You might try out at Love-Struck Vineyards. They host weddings most weekends, and their winery is popular with tourists nearly year around."

"Love-Struck?" Casey suspects the answer, but she asks anyway. "Why is everything in this town named Love?"

"Because the Love family established the town back in the late eighteen hundreds. Members of the extended family own the hotel, the local bank, and the florist. Daniel Love's brood of children runs the vineyard."

Casey goes still, her tea glass poised near her lips. *Daniel Love's brood of children.* Casey's half siblings. She lowers the glass. "Is there someone in specific I should ask for at Love-Struck?"

"I'm not sure. I would just ask for the manager." Ruthie wanders off again to check on the customers at the counter.

Casey finishes her meal, pays the check, and walks across the street to the Red Robin Inn. The small, well-appointed lobby features heavy moldings, rich wall colors, and handsome furnishings. She books a courtyard room, but check-in time is not until four o'clock, which leaves her the afternoon to kill.

Returning to her car, Casey follows Siri's directions five miles outside of town to Love-Struck Vineyard. She passes through impressive brick columns and continues down a winding tree-lined road to a stately stone building.

After she parks and enters the building, she finds groups of customers in a vast room, seated at three of four wooden tasting bars. Casey approaches the vacant bar where a woman is standing with her back to the room, uncorking bottles of wine.

Casey clears her throat. "Excuse me. Is the manager in?"

Bottle in hand, the woman turns to face her. Her name tag identifies her as Ada Love. "I'm one of the owners. How can I help you?"

One of the owners? Ada Love? Is she my half sister? Other than being of similar age, they look nothing alike. Ada's luscious dark hair, the color of rich expresso, is in stark contrast to Casey's golden waves. Ada's eyes are reddish brown, like cognac, while Casey's are a pale olive hue. Ada's lips are pouty. Casey has a dimpled chin.

Casey eases onto a barstool. "I was wondering if you're hiring."

"Do you know anything about wine?" Ada asks, twisting the corkscrew.

Casey grins. "Only that I like to drink it."

Ada doesn't respond to her joke. The cork pops, and she sets down the bottle. "Have you ever waited tables?"

"No. But I'm a fast learner."

"Sorry. We're looking for someone with experience," Ada says, picking up another wine bottle.

Casey leans into the bar. "Look. I really need this job. I'm a hard worker, and I promise I won't let you down."

Ada presses her pouty lips thin. "Sorry. But I don't hire girls like you."

Casey sits back, shocked. "Are you stereotyping me? You don't even know me."

"I know guys go nuts over perky blondes who bat their baby blue eyes at them." She jabs the corkscrew at Casey. "I don't need your kind of trouble."

"I should file a complaint against you to the department of labor. But I don't need *your* kind of trouble." Casey slides off the barstool to her feet. "By the way. They're green."

Ada looks up, as though shocked to see her still standing there. "What's green?"

"My eyes. They're green, not blue."

Ada slams down the bottle. "I don't care what color your eyes are. I'm not hiring you."

"I wouldn't work here if you paid me a million bucks an hour." Casey spins on her heels and marches across the room. An attractive guy sees her coming and opens the door for her. She brushes past him and heads toward the parking lot.

The guy comes after her. "Hey, Goldilocks! Wait up!"

Casey keeps walking. When she reaches her car, he jumps in front of her, preventing her from opening the door.

"What happened back there? Did my sister make you angry?"

His sister? Could this cute guy be my brother? Casey studies him more closely. He's older than her by a few years. Early thirties, she guesses. Waves cascade over his forehead, more sandy-colored than gold, and he has the same pale eyes and cleft chin. "I was asking about a job. She's looking for someone with experience."

He snickers. "Ada's insecure. Pretty girls like you are a threat. Come back inside. Let me talk to her."

"That's okay. I'm not the right fit for the job," Casey says, and is disappointed when he doesn't argue.

"You might try at Foxtail Farm." He sweeps an arm off to the right. "It's the next vineyard over. Ollie, the new owner, is opening a tasting room cafe in June. She may be hiring. Ollie is nothing like my sister. She's super cool. I imagine she'd be fun to work for." He holds his hand out to her. "I'm Sheldon Love, by the way."

His hand is warm and soft in hers. "Casey Hobbs. Nice to meet you."

Casey suddenly wants to know more about her brother, this older guy who looks so much like her. But she's not ready to reveal her identity yet. Getting in her car, she starts the engine and rolls down the window. She waves as she drives off and he yells, "See you soon, Goldilocks!"

Returning to the highway, Casey takes a right in the direction opposite town, and drives two miles to Foxtail Farm. She parks at the entrance and gets out of the car, admiring the view—neat rows of grapevines stretching as far as the eye can see in nearly every direction. She inhales a deep breath. The air smells like springtime. Fresh growth and new beginnings.

During the height of her mother's career, they'd owned a second home in The Hamptons. Casey lived for the summer months when they would spend most weekends sailing and soaking up the sun by the pool. She never felt like she belonged in the city. New York's hustle and bustle, instead of energizing her like most city dwellers, made her nervous. Perhaps Lovely is where she was meant to be. Is it possible mountain living is in her blood?

Back in the car, she follows the black split-rail fence to a large gray farmhouse and bangs the knocker on the yellow front door. A striking young woman with two pencils protruding from a messy bun answers the door.

"I'm looking for Ollie," Casey says.

"I'm Ollie. Who are you?"

"Casey Hobbs. I'm interested in any potential jobs you might have available. Sheldon Love suggested I speak to you."

Ollie narrows her aqua eyes, as though skeptical. "Are you a friend of Sheldon's?"

"No, we just met. I'm from New York."

"New York? How did you land in Lovely?"

Casey's throat swells as the words spill from her mouth. "I lost my mother recently. I needed a change."

Ollie's expression softens. "I'm sorry. I can relate. Both my parents died in a fire summer before last. Come on in." She opens the door wider and steps aside.

Casey enters a large foyer and follows Ollie through a dining room to an upscale kitchen with marble countertops, charcoal gray cabinets, and stainless appliances. A pair of open doors allow fresh mountain air to waft in from the screened porch.

Ollie removes two bottled waters from the refrigerator and hands one to Casey. "What sort of job are you looking for?"

Casey shrugs. "Whatever you're offering. I have a degree in graphic design. But I'll pick grapes if necessary."

Ollie laughs. "We won't harvest the grapes until the fall. When you say graphic design, does that mean you can create wine labels and logos?"

"Sure! I worked for a couple of years at a New York firm before I had to quit to take care of my mom."

"Do you know anything about email newsletters?"

"A little. But I'm good at computers. I'm sure I can figure it out."

The sound of loud scratching on the screen door draws them out to the porch. Ollie opens the door and two nearly identical black and white Border collies tumble in.

Casey drops to her knees to pet them. "Aww. They're adorable. What're their names?"

"Rosé and Chardonnay. Chard for short. They're from the same litter."

"Cute." Casey buries her face in one of the dog's fur. She'd begged for a dog as a child, but her mother would never consent. Beverly believed high-rise apartment buildings were the wrong place for pets. "They're so sweet."

Ollie grunts. "They're little menaces. I inherited them from the previous owner. He couldn't take them with him when he moved to Arizona."

"I'm sure he was sad to leave them behind," Casey says, getting to her feet.

"If you're interested, I can show you around," Ollie offers.

"I would love that."

Leaving the dogs on the porch, Ollie and Casey head off down the gravel driveway toward the rear of the property. Ollie shows her the winery, with its enormous stainless tanks and oak barrels, before leading her to the barn and lodge located at the end of the gravel drive.

"The lodge is circa 1900," Ollie explains. "Over the years, the previous owners have used the building for many purposes—as a school, a place of worship, and a meeting house. We've recently completed extensive renovations to convert the building into our tasting room cafe, The Foxhole."

Casey circles the room, admiring the vaulted ceiling and french doors opening onto a covered porch and bluestone terrace. A massive stone fireplace occupies one end, and at the opposite, a metal frame topped with a thick sheet of plywood stretches long.

Ollie notices Casey eyeing the rudimentary table. "This will be our tasting bar. The plywood is temporary. I'm having a live edge slab milled from a black walnut tree. Sadly, we had to cut the tree down to make room for the terrace. The wood is spectacular. The top should be ready any day. I can hardly wait to see it."

Casey gives an appreciative nod. "The room has an edgy feel despite the obvious historic vibe. When's the opening?"

"In early June. If we make it."

"You're going to put Love-Struck out of business."

Ollie stiffens. "I don't consider the Loves my competition. Love-Struck is a wedding destination. Foxtail is a boutique winery." She throws open the doors, and they step out onto the terrace. "You won't find a view like this next door."

Twenty-five yards off the terrace, the landscape descends into a valley, providing an unobstructed view of the Blue Ridge Mountains. "Wow! It's amazing."

"We have richer soil than the Loves, which yields superior wine. And a talented young chef who's going to put The Foxhole on the map."

A petite young woman wearing an apron and a smudge of flour on her cheek emerges from the lodge. "Did I hear someone mention my name?"

Ollie turns to face her. "I was singing your praises as usual. Fiona, meet Casey Hobbs. Casey, this is Fiona Fortnanny."

"Fort who?" Casey giggles. "I'm sorry. I don't think I can pronounce your name."

Fiona laughs. "No worries. I'm used to it. Just call me Fiona."

"Casey is looking for a job," Ollie informs Fiona. "She's originally from New York, and she has a degree in graphic design."

Fiona casts her gaze upward. "An answer to our prayers."

Confusion crosses Casey's face. "I'm sorry. Did I miss something?"

Ollie laughs. "Fiona and I are stretched thin. There's so much left to do before the opening in six weeks. Over coffee this morning, we were saying we needed another one of us, particularly someone with computer and graphic skills."

Fiona spreads her arms wide at Casey. "And here you are. Our savior."

In a warning tone, Ollie says, "If you decide to take the job, you may be called upon to serve wine to customers or wait tables in the cafe until we get our feet on the ground."

Casey beams. "That's fine! I'll do whatever you need."

"Then you're hired." Ollie gives Casey a smack on the back that stings a little, but Casey doesn't care. She really wants this job. Not because of the proximity to the Love family, but because of the camaraderie between these two women. They are building something special here. And she very much wants to be a part of it.

"Any chance you need a place to live? I just rented a small house off Magnolia Avenue, and I'd love to have a roommate to share the expenses." Fiona tells her the rent, which Casey thinks is a bargain compared to the cost of living in New York.

This day couldn't get any better. "I'm in!"

CHAPTER 2

The next morning, when Casey arrives promptly at nine o'clock to see the rental house, Fiona greets her at the door. The adorable cottage, a taupe-colored Cape Cod, features dormer windows and a small front porch with a bench swing. Two bedrooms, each with its own bath, occupy the second floor, and a sunny living room, dining room, and kitchen with breakfast counter take up the first.

"I have so much stuff," Fiona says of the furnishings in the living room. "I can move some things around to make room for your furniture."

The decor is eclectic but tasteful. Casey can hardly take her eyes off the scrumptious Tiffany blue velvet sofa. "That's alright. I only have clothes."

Fiona raises an eyebrow. "No bedding or towels?"

"Nope. I'm making a fresh start. I got rid of all my old baggage."

"Right. Ollie told me about your mom. I'm so sorry."

"Thanks," Casey says, swallowing past the lump in her throat. The sadness, never far away, makes her wonder whether she'll ever feel like her old upbeat self again.

"Is your father still alive?" Fiona asks.

"I never met my father." *What if my father is dead*? Casey wonders. She hasn't considered this scenario until now. She recalls Ruthie saying the vineyard is run by Daniel Love's children. Which could very well mean that Daniel has died and left the vineyard to his children. Then again, it could mean Daniel has retired.

"Gosh! That's tough. Do you have any siblings?"

"Nope. I'm all alone in the world."

Fiona draws herself to her full height. "Well, not anymore. You have Ollie and me now."

Casey smiles. She'd worried about the awkwardness of living with a perfect stranger, but Fiona's friendliness sets her at ease. "Do you think I can find a retailer who will deliver a mattress today?"

"Not in Lovely. You'll have to go to the next town over. Hope Springs has all the big-box stores. And it's only a twenty-minute drive. You can always sleep on the sofa if they can't deliver today."

Casey envisions herself drooling on the gorgeous blue velvet. "Let's hope it doesn't come to that." She moves toward the front door. "I'm off to Hope Springs, then. I guess I'll see you tonight."

Fiona gives her a silver key. "The lock sticks sometimes. Just pull the door toward you and turn hard."

"Got it," Casey says, taking the key from her.

There's not a cloud in the sky, and the morning sun is warm. Casey puts the top down on the Volvo, letting the wind whip through her curls during her scenic drive.

Hope Springs is far bigger than Lovely, but there's only one mattress store in town. After trying out several brands, she settles on an affordable yet comfortable set. While the set is in stock, the store can't deliver it until the following Monday.

She argues with the sales agent. "But today is only Wednesday. Are you sure you can't deliver it sooner? It's an emergency." No way is she sleeping five nights on Fiona's blue velvet sofa.

"Sorry. Monday's the best I can do."

Casey sighs. Maybe Fiona has an air mattress.

At the antique mall down the street, she finds an upholstered headboard, suitable chest of drawers, and nightstand. She convinces the owner to deliver her purchases this afternoon and pays him extra to pick up the mattress set for her.

Bed, Bath, and Beyond is her next stop. She buys a lamp, towels, and bedding, including a comforter set with a gray-and-white geometric design.

Pleased with her success, Casey treats herself to a latte and chicken salad sandwich at Caffeine on the Corner. With time to kill, she window-shops the boutiques on Main Street, pausing for a long time in front of the art supplies store. It's been years since she created anything, and her fingers itch to draw. She enters the store and splurges on a sketch pad and set of seventy-two professional colored pencils.

Casey is stuffing a pillow into her sham early evening when Fiona arrives home from work.

"Honey, I'm home," she calls out from inside the front door.

Casey places the pillow on the bed and hurries down the stairs. "Guess what? I found everything I need in Hope Springs, including a mattress and a bed."

"Awesome! I can't wait to see what you bought. I would give you a high five, but my hands are full." Fiona holds up two recyclable grocery bags. "I stopped at the store on the way home. I'm making you a welcome dinner."

"Here. Let me help." Casey takes a bag from her. "But you don't need to cook me dinner."

Mischief appears on Fiona's lips. "I have an ulterior motive. I've been pondering a new recipe, a chicken and wild rice dish. You get to be my guinea pig."

"In that case, count me in," Casey says and follows Fiona through the downstairs to the kitchen.

Setting the bags on the counter, Fiona removes a bottle of wine and holds it out for Casey to inspect the label. "I hope you approve."

Casey grins. "When it comes to wine, I don't discriminate."

"Well, you'd better start. You're working for a winery now." Fiona rummages through a drawer for a corkscrew.

"I was afraid to tell Ollie I know basically nothing about wine for fear she wouldn't hire me. Maybe you can give me a crash course."

"Sure thing." Fiona pours a splash of white wine into two glasses, handing one to Casey. "No time like the present for your first lesson."

Fiona gives Casey a brief tutorial on the different stages of wine tasting—appearance, aroma or bouquet, mouth feel, and the finish. She eyes Casey's glass. "Now, tell me what you taste."

Casey sips the white liquid. "Wine."

Fiona laughs. "Be more specific. This wine is a Viognier, one of Virginia's signature varietals." She brings her glass to her lips. "I taste peaches, maybe a hint of pear."

Casey sips again. "I taste the pears," she says, although she can't truly identify the flavors on her tongue.

Fiona smiles. "Keep practicing while I start dinner."

As Fiona unloads groceries, Casey takes her wine over to the breakfast counter. She takes several more sips, but it's just wine to her. Perhaps she should stick to the business side of running Foxtail Farm.

"Tell me about the Love family," Casey says. "I met Ada and Sheldon yesterday when I was looking for a job. Is there friction between Ollie and the Loves?"

"What makes you ask that?" Fiona's back is to Casey as she sautés mushrooms at the stove.

"Just a vibe I got from Ollie when I told her Sheldon suggested I talk to her about employment opportunities."

"Sheldon has the hots for Ollie. But she won't admit it. She has a boyfriend. Jamie. You'll meet him soon. He hangs around the farm a lot." Fiona finishes with the mushrooms and joins her at the breakfast counter. "The two older Love brothers are determined to own Foxtail Farm."

Two older Love brothers. More of my half siblings? How many of them are there?

"Why didn't they buy it when it was on the market?" Casey asks.

"Because the previous owner wouldn't sell it to them. The Basses and Loves have been feuding since the families settled here in the late 1800s."

Casey furrows her brow. "Feuding? You mean like the Hatfields and McCoys?"

"Exactly." Fiona pours more wine into their glasses. "Anyway, Hugh and Charles Love did everything possible to sabotage the lodge renovations. They set small fires, interrupted supply deliveries, and interfered with subcontractors' schedules. The contractor, an experienced builder from Hope Springs, reported everything to the sheriff, but he could never pin anything on them. Sly bastards. But Ollie knows it was them. They threatened her to her face, told her they'd ruin her if she didn't sell."

Casey's heart sinks. Her brothers are criminals. She's not sure she wants to know her family. "Poor Ollie. I feel sorry for her."

With a huff, Fiona says, "If anyone can handle them, Ollie can."

Casey remembers what Ollie said about the Loves yesterday. "Is it the rich soil they want?"

"The Loves don't care about winemaking. They want the land for the view. They have in mind to build a luxury resort, complete with spa and golf course."

Casey blinks hard. "A golf course? In the middle of the vineyard? Are their parents involved in the business?"

"I've never met the father, although I've seen him from afar. He's nice looking, but he has a reputation for being a hard-ass. His wife died years ago. Dropped dead from a brain aneurysm on the tennis court."

So my father isn't dead.

"That's so awful," Casey says, and she means it. She's sorry her siblings lost their mother, although the absence of a wife might make it easier for her to approach her father when the time is right.

Fiona finishes her wine and returns to the stove. "I don't know about you, but I'm starving."

"Famished. It smells heavenly. What can I do to help?" Casey asks, pushing off the barstool.

"Why don't you make the salad. The ingredients are in the fridge."

Fiona and Casey work together in companionable silence as they prepare the meal. When dinner is ready, they take their plates outside to the small table on the deck. While they eat, Fiona talks about growing up in Georgia and her dreams of one day starting a cake company.

When dusk settles over them, strings of little white lights outlining the porch railings blink on. Casey lets out a delighted giggle. "It's magic."

Fiona smiles. "They're on a timer. Do you like them?"

"I love them. Do you think you'll stay in Lovely?"

"Maybe. I like it here. Although I want to get married one day and start a family. I'm not sure I'll find my life partner in Lovely."

"I can see where that might be a challenge," Casey says.

"For now, my primary focus is launching The Foxhole. If we're successful, offers from other restaurants might present themselves down the road."

"I know you'll be successful." Casey drags a chunk of sourdough bread through the remaining sauce on her plate. "This was delicious, simple but tasty."

Fiona forks a tiny bite of chicken into her mouth. "Needs a little more sherry. But I'm glad you like it. I'll add it to my growing recipe files. At least now I can stop thinking about this concoction and obsessing about something else."

Casey chuckles. "It's a curse sometimes, pondering ideas for

days, sometimes weeks, until they finally take shape. I'm an illustrator. Ideas have been floating around in my brain since Ollie
mentioned designing a new wine label."

"I'm envious of you being an illustrator. I can't draw a stick
figure. Do you paint as well?"

"A little. But it's been awhile. I haven't created anything since
Mom got sick."

Fiona's face softens. "I'd like to hear about your mom if you
feel like talking about her."

More tears fill Casey's eyes. "I don't think I can. It's too soon."

"I understand." Fiona reaches across the table. "But whenever
you're ready, I'm a good listener."

"That means a lot. Thank you." Casey appreciates her new
roommate's kindness. But the truth is, all her life, Casey has been
known as Beverly Hobbs's daughter. She wants to try being just
Casey for a change.

CHAPTER 3

Ollie greets Casey at the door with a cup of coffee and shows her to a paneled library featuring two desks, shelves packed with books, and a stone fireplace with a landscape painting of the vineyard above the mantel on the far wall.

"Sorry we have to share. I eventually plan to create office space in the winery, but this is all I have for now."

"No worries. This is fine."

Ollie appears relieved. "Working together will make it easier for us to collaborate on projects. You'll have the office to yourself most of the time anyway. Now that I'm turning the computer work over to you, I plan to spend my time in the vineyard." She heads for the door. "Make yourself at home. There's a Keurig in the kitchen with a variety of flavored K-cups. Call me if you need anything."

After settling in at her new desk, Casey devotes the morning to designing a flashy newsletter for their extensive list of followers, announcing the vineyard under new ownership and the upcoming grand opening of their tasting room and cafe.

Ollie is impressed when Casey shows her the newsletter. "Do you know anything about web design?"

"A lot, actually. I love designing websites."

"Cool! Ours needs a major update." Ollie shares the sign-in credentials, and Casey spends the next couple of hours poking around.

When she's finished, she goes in search of Ollie to report her recommendations. She finds her new boss having a late lunch at the kitchen island.

Casey brews a Chai Latte on the Keurig and sits down beside her. "About the website . . . You need more than an update. I suggest a complete overhaul. I assume you'll want to feature The Foxhole with links to a restaurant reservation system. Do you envision an e-commerce platform to sell wine directly to clients?"

"Yes, and yes! How long will the redesign take?"

"That depends. You mentioned new branding for your labels. If you want to incorporate those designs into the website, we'll wait to launch until they're ready."

Ollie stands and walks her empty soup bowl to the sink. "How soon before we have a concept for the rebranding?"

Casey sips her latte. "Again, that depends on how long it takes me to come up with a design that wows you. But I have something in mind. Why don't I sketch it for you? That'll at least give us a starting point."

"That'd be great." Ollie rinses the bowl and turns to face Casey. "You've only been here a few hours, but I'm tempted to give you a raise."

Casey grins. "You never said. How much *are* you paying me?"

Ollie's hand flies to her mouth. "I'm so sorry. I have so many details floating around in my head, I can't keep them all straight. You were very trusting to show up today without knowing how much you'll be earning."

Casey shrugs. "I need the job. And I felt like I'd enjoy working here."

"I hope you do. I plan to pay you well, so you don't want to leave." The amount Ollie presents makes Casey's eyes bulge.

"You'll also receive other compensation," Ollie says as an introduction to her employee benefits.

When Ollie leaves to work the vineyard, Casey retrieves her art supplies from the office and takes them to the wicker rockers on the back porch. She's still working hours later when she senses someone watching her. She cranes her neck to see a boyishly handsome young man peering over her shoulder.

"She's adorable," he says about Casey's illustration of a female fox with bright blue eyes, long eyelashes, and a sly smile.

Casey smiles up at him. "Thanks."

"Ollie will love her."

"I hope so."

He plops down in the rocker next to Casey. "May I?" he asks, easing the sketch pad from her hands. He studies the illustration and suggests a couple of subtle additions. When he hands her back the pad, she makes the changes, which yield striking results.

"You have a good eye," Casey says. "Are you an artist?"

"Nope. A realtor. I'm Ollie's boyfriend, Jamie."

"Nice to meet you, Jamie." Casey closes the sketch pad and shifts in her seat to face him. "I'm Casey, her new graphic designer. Ollie's amazing. Have you two been dating long?"

"Only about six months. But I'm certain she's the one. I'm thinking of asking her to marry me," Jamie says, his ice-blue eyes twinkling.

Casey senses a hesitancy in his voice. "Is something holding you back?"

"Ollie doesn't want children. I always assumed I'd be a father. I never thought much about it until now. The idea of not having a family leaves me with an empty feeling inside."

His willingness to speak so openly to a total stranger surprises Casey. "Why doesn't Ollie want children?"

Jamie rolls his eyes. "She thinks she's too old."

Casey guesses Jamie to be closer in age to Casey than to Ollie. "Age shouldn't matter. Not with the infertility treatments available these days."

"Ollie knows that. She's using it as an excuse. She's more interested in her vineyard than having children. And I get that. Her ambition is one thing I admire most about her."

"Maybe she'll change her mind, once she's gotten over the newness of owning a vineyard."

"That's what I'm hoping."

Chard and Rosé come racing up the driveway from the barn. They paw at the screen door, and when Jamie lets them in, the Border collies chase each other around the porch.

Casey laughs. "What's with the zoomies?"

"They're hungry. Ollie can never remember to feed them. She lets them run wild. I've warned her, they're gonna get hit by a car one day." Jamie shrugs. "If she can't take care of her dogs, maybe she would make a lousy mom." He slaps his thigh and the dogs scamper behind him into the kitchen.

He's no sooner left than Casey spots Ollie striding toward the house in cowboy boots, faded jeans, and a sweat-soaked T-shirt. She wears a western-style straw hat over her dark chocolate hair, which she's woven into a single braid down her back.

Jamie returns from feeding the dogs. He opens the door for Ollie, and when he gives her a peck on the cheek, she stiffens. Is it possible Ollie's feelings for Jamie aren't as strong as his are for her?

"Wait until you see Casey's drawings," Jamie says, dragging Ollie across the porch.

Casey hands Ollie the sketch pad and watches closely for her response.

"A mascot! She's absolutely perfect." Ollie hugs the pad to her chest. "You're a godsend, Casey." She casts her eyes heavenward. "I'm convinced our guardian angel mothers met in heaven and arranged for us to work together."

Casey's eyes well, and Ollie says, "I didn't mean to make you cry."

She fingers away her tears. "I'm sorry. I never know when something will set me off. And that was a lovely thing to say. I'd like to believe it's true."

Ollie hands her back the sketch pad. "Tell me more about your concept."

"Well, I'm thinking each wine bottle will have a different label. The fox's expression and pose will reflect the mood of the wine."

"The mood of the wine? That's an interesting perception." Ollie toys with her braid as she paces the length of the porch. "You might be on to something." She stops walking and looks up at Casey. "Are you in a hurry to leave? Or can you stay for a little wine tasting?"

"I can stay," Casey says. "But I warn you, I know little about wine."

"Then it's time you learn. Fiona has some bottles at the lodge. I'll let her know we're coming," Ollie says and thumbs off a text.

"I'm coming with you," Jamie says, falling in line behind them as they exit the porch.

Ollie laughs. "I can always count on your tastebuds, Jamie."

Casey increases her pace to keep up with Ollie. "I owe you an apology. I should've been up-front with you regarding my lack of knowledge about wine. Fiona tried to teach me how to taste last night. I failed the lesson."

Ollie gives her a sidelong glance. "No worries. Developing your taste takes time."

Fiona is setting up bottles and glasses on the makeshift tasting bar when they arrive. As she pops corks, Ollie repeats the stages of wine tasting Casey learned from Fiona. Only she goes into more depth, and Casey feels overwhelmed.

"Let's start with this white." Ollie pours a splash into four glasses and passes them around. "Pinot grigios tend to be more citrusy."

While the others talk of color and bouquet, Casey closes her eyes and sips the crisp wine.

"Well," Ollie says. "What do you think, Casey?"

Casey opens her eyes. "This wine invigorates me. I feel alive, like I'm walking through a pine forest on a snowy winter's morning. I imagine the fox on this label having vivid orange fur and bright blue eyes." She rips a clean sheet of paper from her pad and makes notes with an orange pencil.

"Try the Viognier," Ollie says, pouring a clear wine from another bottle and sliding the glass toward her. "Viognier is French in origin but has done well in the Virginia mountains. Viognier vines don't hit their peak until around twenty years. Most of ours are in their late teens. The wine they produce is already excellent. I can't wait to see what's down the pike. It's drier than one might expect, and the flavor is intense."

Casey takes a sip and then another. "I like it." She leaves the bar and strolls with glass in hand around the room, pausing to look out the french doors. Her glass is empty when she turns back toward the others. "This fox is clever and purposeful. She knows what she wants. The world is her oyster." Casey reaches the bar and jots notes on her pad. "I haven't figured out her position, but she's giving us a knowing wink."

When Casey looks up from her notes, the others are staring at her.

"You're really good at this," Fiona says. "Try one of the reds."

Ollie hands her a glass of purple-colored wine. Casey tastes the wine. "Hmm. Nice. This fox is demure but sexy. She's curled up by a fire on a cold winter's night. Her eyelids are droopy. Her fur soft."

"That's the Cabernet Sauvignon. Try this Petit Verdot." Ollie slides another glass toward her. "It's bold and full-bodied. I'd never tasted it until I came to Virginia. But it's quickly become my favorite."

Casey brings the glass to her lips. "I taste blackberries and something spicy," she says, proud of herself for identifying the flavors. "It's delicious. And smooth." Her face warms. "This fox is seductive. Her eyes are smoldering as she slinks along on her prow."

Ollie reads over Casey's shoulder as she makes notes on her paper. "Earlier today, you said you wanted to wow me. Well, I'm wowed. This campaign is going to be outstanding. It's exactly what I was hoping for."

Casey beams up at her. "I'm glad."

"I'm surprised you draw by hand," Jamie says. "In today's world, aren't most graphics created on a computer?"

Casey drains the rest of the Petit Verdot. "Every artist has their process. I connect better with my subjects if I draw them first. I'll eventually convert them into illustrations in Adobe Illustrator to use for printed materials and online marketing."

Fiona's eyes are on Ollie when she asks, "Do we want to incorporate the fox in The Foxhole label? Or is that too much?"

Ollie chews on her lip as she considers the question. "I can see our mascot peeping out of a hole. Yes! Let's use the fox but somehow differentiate it from the wine labels."

"I'll give it some thought," Casey says, scribbling more notes.

"Are we gonna name this mascot?" Jamie asks, helping himself to more wine.

Ollie cuts her eyes at him, as though she disapproves, but Fiona and Casey both jump at the idea.

Casey drums her fingers on the plywood. "The name should begin with *F*. Like Frances or Fanny."

Fiona giggles. "We could call her *Fiona*. Just kidding. What about Felicia? Or Frankie?"

"If we're going to name her, we have to come up with the right name," Ollie says, and while they finish the wine, they toss around possibilities.

"That's enough. We don't have to decide on a name today." Ollie gathers the empty bottles and takes them into the kitchen.

Casey whispers to Fiona. "I'm too tipsy to drive home. Do you have a buzz?"

Fiona presses her fingers to her lips to hide her smile. "Yes!"

Ollie emerges from the kitchen. "I can't let you drive home after all that wine."

Casey wonders if she overheard them talking. "We can call an Uber."

Ollie laughs. "You're in the middle of nowhere, Casey. Closest Uber driver lives in Hope Springs. You'll stay for dinner while you sober up. I'll roast some vegetables from my garden, and I have some sausages I can throw on the grill."

"That sounds yummy," Fiona says. "I'll help you."

On the way to the house, Casey blurts out, "I know! Why don't we call our mascot Fancy?"

Ollie's hand flies to her chest. "Fancy the Fox. I absolutely love it."

Fiona and Jamie voice their approval.

Ollie slips her arm through Casey's. "I'm not sure who sent you or where you came from, my little creative genius, but I'm glad you found your way here."

Casey hasn't worked in three years, and her drawing skills are rusty. She can come up with ideas all day long. She just hopes she can deliver a finished product that will please her new boss.

CHAPTER 4

Casey's worries about her inability to produce fresh content prove to be unnecessary. Her creative juices, flowing like never before, transport her visions of Fancy the Fox directly to her fingertips. Not only does she dream about the mascot at night, she carries her around on her shoulder all throughout the day.

After two weeks of meticulous work, Casey deems her designs ready for Ollie's feedback. She spreads the drawings out on the round dining room table and holds her breath while Ollie scrutinizes each one.

When she finally looks up from the drawings, Ollie says, "They're brilliant, Casey. I couldn't choose a favorite if I had to."

Ollie picks up The Foxhole drawing—a bird's-eye view of Fancy peeking out from a hole in the ground, her orange fur vivid against the yellow-green blades of grass. "Have you shown this to Fiona?"

"Not yet. I wanted your approval first."

"Well, you certainly have that." Ollie returns the drawing to the table. "Where do we go from here?"

"I'll create digital files from the drawings. Once you sign off on those, we can order our print products. In the meantime, I'll begin working on the website redesign."

Ollie draws her in for a half hug. "I'm impressed, Casey. Your work is excellent."

A feeling of satisfaction settles over Casey as she gathers up the drawings and floats back to her office. She adores her job and new friends. She never realized how much she missed the companionship of peers during her three-year break from life. She came to Lovely to find her father. But she's discovered so much more in the short time she's been here. She'll eventually attempt to meet Daniel Love. But she's in no hurry.

Casey and Fiona share a unique bond, as if they've known each other a lifetime instead of a few short weeks. She feels at ease with Jamie as well. He stops by the farm most afternoons to see Ollie. She's rarely around, but Casey is usually working on the porch. He helps himself to a glass of sweet tea or lemonade and joins her for a chat.

Jamie often expresses his frustration over what he refers to as Ollie's obsession with the Loves.

"Describe this obsession you keep talking about," Casey finally says one day in early May. "I haven't seen this side of her."

"Then you haven't been listening," Jamie says. "She's always ranting and raving about the Loves."

Casey lifts an eyebrow. "Can you blame her after the way they've treated her?"

"Not at all. I don't get why she still allows Sheldon on her property."

"Sheldon seems like a nice enough guy."

"The apple never falls far from the tree, Casey. Sheldon is totally in on their efforts to buy this farm. He's the good cop to his brothers' bad cop routine."

While Casey disagrees with Jamie, she doesn't argue. She is fruit from the same tree, yet she doesn't have a mean bone in her body.

When Casey questions Jamie about his background, he admits

to being a screwup in college. "I barely graduated from UVA with a degree in history. I never gave my future much thought. I always assumed I'd take over our family's real estate firm when my dad retires. I don't *mind* selling houses, although it's not my passion. I envy Ollie all this." He spreads his arms wide at the vineyard. "Being out in the wide open with an abundance of fresh air and sunshine. Who knows? Maybe I'll quit selling real estate and work on the farm once we're married."

Casey has trouble imagining this scenario. The more she's around Ollie and Jamie, the more she's convinced they're all wrong for each other. Jamie is like a love-sick teenager, and Ollie barely acknowledges his presence.

"Why does Ollie string Jamie along when she's clearly not into him?" Casey asks Fiona on a Sunday night in mid-May. They're lounging on the velvet sofa, watching a series on Netflix, a cashmere throw tucked around their legs and a bowl of popcorn nestled between them.

"Good question. I don't get it. I've tried talking to Ollie about it, but she's made it clear the subject is off limits. These past few years have been difficult for Ollie, with a failed marriage and losing her parents. I wonder if she's using Jamie as a safety net."

"Wait! What?" Casey says, struggling to sit up on the sofa. "I didn't know she'd been married before."

"Yep. To the foreman at her family's vineyard. He was a much older guy. Ollie was a bit of a wild child, and her husband made the mistake of trying to tame her before she was ready to settle down."

Casey slides back down under the blanket. "So, you think that, because Jamie is so clearly devoted to her, he'll never hurt her?"

"Right. *And* if she stays with him, she won't have to acknowledge her attraction to Sheldon."

Casey chews on a fingernail. "Maybe. But I predict Ollie will eventually see the light."

She envisions a broken heart in Jamie's future. When that happens, she'll be there to see him through. As his friend, not his rebound person. Although, maybe one day, something more will come of their friendship.

Sheldon, too, visits Foxtail often with fabricated excuses to see Ollie—mostly warnings about her dogs crossing the property line onto their land. Casey watches Ollie closely whenever Sheldon is around. Despite Ollie's curt comments and icy glares, an undeniable attraction exists between them.

On Tuesday morning the last day in May, Casey is at her desk in the study when she hears tires crunching gravel followed by the slamming of a car door. Peeking out the window, she sees Sheldon storming up the sidewalk.

Pushing back from her desk, Casey hurries to the front door, swinging it open to find a flustered Sheldon reaching for the knocker.

"Where's Ollie?" he says in a demanding tone.

"I'm not sure. Around here somewhere."

"I'm here," Ollie says, emerging from the kitchen. "What's wrong now, Sheldon?"

"My brothers called animal control. They trapped the dogs and have taken them to the pound."

Ollie tenses, fingers balling into fists at her side. "Damn it! Why did you let this happen?"

Sheldon's nostrils flare. "Why did *you* let this happen? I've warned you repeatedly about Chard and Rosé."

Ollie snatches her purse off the coat rack by the door. "Where are my dogs?"

"At the animal shelter in Hope Springs." Sheldon dangles his keys. "I'll drive you."

"I can drive myself," Ollie says, brushing past him. "Casey, you're coming with me."

Sheldon follows her out with Casey on his heels.

"I'm coming too. Let me help you, Ollie. My brothers issued the complaint. I'll tell them it was all a mistake."

"Fine. But we need to hurry before they euthanize them. You

can drive." Ollie changes directions, heading toward Sheldon's Range Rover.

Ollie climbs into the back, leaving the passenger seat for Casey. An awkward silence settles over the car. Casey thinks Ollie is being melodramatic. Surely the animal control people won't euthanize the dogs. Or will they? She pulls out her phone, but her Google search for information on impounded dogs yields few results.

As they approach Hope Springs, Casey locates the address for the local animal control center and plugs it into her Maps app.

A cantankerous older woman with a mop of gray curls and reading glasses dangling from a beaded chain around her neck greets them at the front desk. "May I help you?"

"I'm here for my dogs," Ollie snaps. "They've been wrongfully impounded."

Sheldon steps forward, nudging Ollie out of the way. "There's been a mistake. I'm Sheldon Love from over in Lovely. My brothers have a vendetta against our neighbor, and they're taking it out on her dogs. Chard and Rosé have done nothing wrong. I'm happy to pay the fines." He removes his wallet from his back pocket and hands the woman a credit card.

"Young man." The woman levels her gaze at him. "Using one's pets as pawns in one's disagreements with family and friends and, in this case, neighbors is immoral. You forced those innocent animals to endure unnecessary cruelty." She catches herself. "Not that we mistreated them. But they were undoubtedly frightened at being caged and removed from their home."

"I understand, ma'am. And I'm terribly sorry," Sheldon says, sounding sincere.

"Don't apologize to me. You need to make it up to those poor dogs." She wags her finger at Sheldon. "Do you understand me?"

A smile tugs at Sheldon's lips, but he keeps a straight face. "Yes, ma'am. We will. As soon as we get them home."

The woman lifts a phone receiver. "I'll have them brought up."

Five minutes later, an attendant leads the dogs out on leashes, and Sheldon herds them out to the car.

"You handled that woman well," Casey says to Sheldon on the way back to Lovely.

Sheldon raises his voice an octave, mimicking the woman. "Don't apologize to me. You need to make it up to those poor dogs."

Casey laughs. "You sound just like her."

In the same high-pitched tone, Sheldon goes on about animal cruelty. Casey belly laughs until tears stream down her cheeks. When she glimpses Ollie glaring stone-faced at her from the back seat, Casey stops laughing and straightens. Her opinion of Ollie drops a notch. Sheldon just bailed her dogs out of the pound, and she hasn't even thanked him.

"We need to figure out a way to keep the dogs off the Loves' property," Casey ventures despite Ollie's obvious annoyance at the situation.

"We live in the country," Ollie snaps. "Last I checked, there's no leash law outside the city limits."

Sheldon seeks her out in the rearview mirror. "I agree with Casey. If you don't restrain the dogs, my brothers will call animal control again."

"I'll worry about my dogs. You take care of your brothers."

Casey cringes at the hostility in Ollie's tone and doesn't say another word on the way home.

When they arrive back at Foxtail Farm, Ollie jumps out of the car and books it up to the house, leaving Casey to handle the dogs. She casts Sheldon an apologetic look. "Thanks. I'm sure Ollie appreciates what you did. She's just a little worked up right now."

Sheldon offers Casey a sympathetic smile. "You don't need to make excuses for her. She has plenty of reason not to trust my family."

"Still. She could've been nicer."

Casey lets the dogs out of the back and leads them to the

screen porch. She joins Ollie in the kitchen where she's making coffee. "You were kinda hard on Sheldon. He was only trying to help."

Ollie spins on her heels to face her. "You don't understand, Casey. Hugh and Charles Love just took their crusade to the next level." She falls back against the counter. "They want this land. Sheldon's nice guy routine is just an act. The Love brothers, all three of them, are ganging up against me."

Casey believes Sheldon is trying to make peace, but now is not the time to voice her opinion.

Ollie returns her attention to the coffeemaker. "You're right about the dogs though. I need to do something. I could build a kennel for them, but I hate to keep them locked up."

"Why not give the previous owner a call? Maybe he can offer you some advice on how to handle the dogs."

"That's an excellent idea." Ollie grabs her phone off the counter and steps outside to make the call.

She's on the porch for a long time, pacing and talking and twirling a strand of her long hair. When she finally comes back inside, she's wearing a wide smile. "Melvin says the dogs are highly trained. He gave me his trainer's contact information. I spoke briefly with Ennis Rawlings. He lives over near Charlottesville. I'm dropping the dogs off in the morning for a tuneup. When I pick them up in two weeks, he'll show me how to handle them."

"That's wonderful," Casey says, offering her a high five. "For you and the dogs."

Ollie lets out a sigh of relief. "I'm sorry about earlier, Casey. I'm worked up about a number of things. I'm terrified the opening next week will be a flop. If the vineyard doesn't make it, I'll have to sell the farm to the Loves."

"I realize you're under pressure. But you have Fiona and me on your team. We won't let you fail."

Ollie's phone vibrates with an incoming call. She answers and listens for a minute. "I'm on my way," she says, pocketing her phone.

"Let's go." She waves Casey on as she heads for the porch. "They're delivering the top for the tasting bar."

Casey has to jog to keep up with Ollie's pace on the way to the lodge. They arrive to find three deliverymen staring down at the walnut slab and scratching their heads.

"Is there a problem?" Ollie asks, brushing them out of the way.

Casey peers over Ollie's shoulder at the deep groove scratches in the rich walnut wood.

Ollie looks up at them. "How did this happen?"

The head deliveryman says, "We don't know, ma'am. The scratches weren't there when we loaded it on the truck last night."

Ollie's face darkens to a deep red hue. "The Love brothers did this."

Casey sneaks out the door before Ollie goes ballistic.

The rest of the week passes in a flurry of activity. When a shipment of furniture arrives the following morning, Fiona and Casey spend the afternoon helping Ollie arrange chairs and tables and umbrellas. Fiona tweaks her menu items and trains her new staffers. Ollie makes the cafe homier with potted plants and contemporary wall art. And Casey prepares to launch the website and prints hundreds of copies of fliers for advertising.

The technician from the countertop company returns late Friday afternoon to install the refinished walnut slab on the tasting bar.

"It's gorgeous," Casey says, running her hand across the smooth wood.

"A real showpiece," Fiona adds.

Ollie grunts. "No thanks to the Love brothers. I can't wait to see what that family has in store for the opening."

The team expects a slow start to the soft opening week, but

disappointment sets in when not a single customer shows up on Monday for lunch.

"Maybe you need to do a better job of getting the word out," Jamie suggests.

"And I know just how to do it." Casey grabs a stack of flyers and spends the rest of Monday afternoon handing them out to business owners in town, asking them to please let their customers know The Foxhole is now open for lunch every day from eleven until three. Despite her efforts, only a few groups of two and three show up on Tuesday.

Sheldon stops by to check on them around one o'clock. When he sees Ollie's distraught face, he takes a stack of flyers from the checkout counter. "Come with me, Goldilocks," he says, motioning for Casey to follow him outside to his Range Rover.

"Where are we going?" Casey asks as he peels off down the gravel driveway.

He flashes a toothy grin. "To poach customers from my family."

Casey's mouth falls open. "How will you do that?"

"You'll see." He drives up the road to where a long line of cars is waiting at the entrance to Love-Struck vineyards. "It's like this every day. Our food isn't even that great."

Casey's eyes widen. "So when they can't get into the restaurant where they want to eat, they go to the place next door."

"Exactly." He parks on the side of the road, and Casey trails along behind him as he moves from car to car, telling the hungry patrons there's no waiting line at the new hot spot cafe down the road. One by one, the cars pull out of the line and drive off toward Foxtail Farm.

As they rush back to the Foxhole, Casey sends Fiona and Ollie a text alerting them that customers are on the way. Jamie is there when they arrive. He and Sheldon pitch in to help serve. When the crowd finally dies down around three o'clock, they've fed twenty-five groups.

After resetting the kitchen for the next day, Fiona treats

everyone to key lime pie and coffee on the terrace as they assess their performance. Much to their relief, they discover only a few minor issues they need to work through.

"What's your plan for the official grand opening on Saturday?" Sheldon asks, his eyes on Ollie as he forks off a bite of key lime pie.

Ollie shrugs. "We don't really have one. We're not planning a ribbon cutting ceremony, if that's what you're asking."

Sheldon savors the pie and wipes his lips. "A grand opening is supposed to be a party to draw in the local community and show them your stuff."

Ollie looks across the table at Casey. "Do you think it's too late?"

"Not if we get right on it," Casey says. "I can print and hand deliver invitations."

"Our firm has a list of local businesses," Jamie says. "I'm happy to share their addresses."

"That would be great," Casey says.

"My friend has a small bluegrass band," Sheldon says. "Want me to see if he's available on Saturday?"

Jamie's face reddens. "Well, my friend owns an inflatable company. You can rent a giant slide for the kids."

Ollie pushes abruptly back from the table. "Yes, to the bluegrass band. No to the inflatable. This isn't a kid's event. For now, getting the word out is the most pressing issue." She pats the top of Casey's head. "Come on. Let's go up to the house. We can brainstorm on the invitations."

"In hindsight, we should have organized a full-on marketing campaign for the launch," Casey says, as they leave the lodge.

"I agree. Do you know how to tackle something like that?"

"I do," Casey says with a vigorous head nod. "Let's get through the grand opening. And I'll get right on it starting on Monday."

Ollie and Casey work well into the night designing the invitations. Early the next morning, Casey drives over to a quick print shop in Hope Springs and orders two hundred copies. Once she receives the list of local businesses from Jamie, she sets about hand delivering them. She's uncertain what to do about the Loves. Inviting the entire family would be a goodwill gesture, a step toward ending the feud.

She consults Ollie. "Since they're our neighbors, shouldn't we invite the entire Love family?"

Ollie spins around in her desk chair. "No way! No Loves."

"But—"

"No buts, Casey. The grand opening is a public event. If the Loves show up, we'll be hospitable to them. But I won't go out on a limb to make nice to them." Ollie turns back around to face her computer, ending the discussion.

As Saturday draws near, Casey finds herself hoping Daniel Love will attend the opening. If he doesn't show up, she'll have to figure out another way to approach him. The time has come for them to meet.

Saturday at noon, as guests arrive for the opening, Casey keeps her eyes peeled for Daniel Love. But The Foxhole is soon swamped with locals of all ages, and she's too busy hustling about to be on the lookout. She's on the way to the kitchen with an empty tray of Fiona's sweet potato ham biscuits when a gentleman waves her down. "Excuse me, miss!"

She recognizes him from his social media pics, although Daniel Love is far more handsome in person. He's overdressed in a navy blazer and cream-colored linen pants, yet his attire fits him. He carries an air of wealth and privilege with snowy hair and skin tanned golden from the sun.

Standing beside him is a younger man who looks enough like Daniel to be his son, only his permanent scowl distracts from his good looks.

"Can I help you, sir?" Casey asks.

"Great job on the opening," Daniel says. "I'm curious about the owner. Would you mind pointing her out to me?"

Casey's eyes travel across the room to Ollie, who is wearing a cobalt-blue silk sheath that clings to her trim figure. "She's over by the fireplace. Dark hair, blue dress."

Daniel follows her gaze. "She's stunning," he says with a nod of approval before turning his attention back to Casey. "And you? What's your name? You look oddly familiar."

Odd is right. Looking at him creeps her out. But in a good way. He's an older, male version of herself. The dimpled chin is the same, as are the pale olive eyes, only his are lined with crow's feet.

Casey tucks the tray under one arm and extends the opposite hand. "I'm Casey Hobbs, graphic designer for Foxtail Farm."

Daniel's stoic expression gives nothing away. "The only Hobbs I ever knew was Beverly Hobbs, the morning show host. Dare I ask if you're related? That would be quite the coincidence."

Not a coincidence at all, Casey thinks. "Beverly is . . . was my mother."

Daniel's body stills, but she can see the wheels in motion behind those familiar eyes. "Excuse us a minute," Daniel says to his son. Taking Casey by the arm, he leads her out to the edge of the terrace. "Beverly is dead? What happened to her?"

"She died from cancer in early April. How well did you know her?"

"We were once close. But that was years ago, and we lost touch. I kept up with her through *The Good Morning Show.* I was surprised when she retired."

"The producers forced her out," Casey says. "They replaced her for someone much younger."

Daniel's face darkens. "That must have been hard for her."

Casey nods. "She never recovered from the blow to her ego."

"Poor Beverly. She deserved better." Daniel studies Casey's face closely. "When were you born?"

"In March of 1995. Why do you ask?" She already knows the answer. He's putting the puzzle pieces together. This is easier than she expected.

"Just curious. I can't believe Beverly finally got married. She swore she never would."

Tears sting Casey's eyes, and she looks down at the bluestone terrace. "She never did."

"Then who's your father?" Daniel asks, his voice a whisper.

Sucking in a deep breath, she looks up and into his eyes. "I believe you are."

CHAPTER 5

Daniel's shoulders sag as he expels the air from his lungs. "I would argue, if not for the remarkable resemblance. If you know who I am, why haven't you contacted me?"

"I didn't find out about you until after Mom died. She left a letter for me, explaining why she kept your identity a secret. She wanted to protect you, for the sake of your family."

A wistful expression softens his features. "Are you here, in Lovely, because of me? Did you come here to find me?"

Tearing her eyes away from Daniel, she fixates on an attractive brunette wearing a red polka dotted dress across the terrace. "That is why I originally came to Virginia. But I got caught up in my new job. We've been busy preparing for the launch. And I've been trying to figure out a way to approach you. I didn't come here to complicate your life. I just wanted to meet you. I don't expect anything from you."

His son appears in the doorway and calls out to him. "Come on, Dad. Let's go."

Daniel holds up a finger, signaling for his son to wait a minute. "I'd like to see you again. We have much to talk about. Can I have your number?" he asks, sliding his phone out of the inside pocket of his blue blazer.

She recites the number, and he thumbs it into his contacts. "I'll be in touch."

He starts off and then turns back toward her. "We should keep this between us for now. My children—"

She holds up a hand to silence him. "Say no more. Sheldon and I are friends. I'm worried about how he will take the news."

Daniel squeezes her arm and smiles at her. "We'll figure it out. I'm glad to know you, Goldilocks." When she flinches beneath his touch, he says, "What is it? Did I say something wrong?"

"Sheldon calls me Goldilocks," she says in a soft voice.

Daniel chuckles. "I'm not surprised. Your hair is . . ."

Casey smooths back her waves. "Out of control?"

"I was going to say lovely. As are you. I'll be in touch soon."

Casey's heart sinks as she watches him saunter away. He is so . . . so unexpected. Charismatic, a successful man of the world, yet endearing. She swoons as she remembers his words. *I was going to say lovely. As are you.* No wonder her mother fell for him. Beverly, the glamorous morning show hostess, could have had any man she wanted. But Daniel was the only man she ever truly loved.

Casey's gaze shifts, and she notices Fiona staring at her from inside the doors. Is Fiona angry at Casey? Or is her expression one of suspicion?

That evening, Casey and Fiona go for celebratory drinks at their favorite hangout in town. During the short walk to Magnolia Avenue, Fiona says, "I saw you talking to Daniel Love on the terrace earlier. Since when do you know the patron saint of Love-Struck Vineyards?" Her tone is nonchalant, but her blue eyes watch closely for Casey's reaction.

"Since today," Casey says with a straight face.

"Ha. Could've fooled me. You two appeared to be having an

intense conversation. I hope Ollie didn't see you fraternizing with the enemy."

Casey is tempted to tell her new best friend the truth. It's not every day a girl meets her biological father for the first time. However, while she trusts Fiona, she told Daniel she'd keep their relationship between them for now. "He was complimenting us on a job well done with the cafe. He seems like a nice person."

"Don't let him fool you," Fiona says in a warning tone. "He can only be but so nice with Hugh and Charles for sons. You should've seen Hugh today, strutting around like he owned the place while you were talking with his father on the terrace."

"How can you be sure that was Hugh and not Charles?"

"Because he introduced himself to me," Fiona says. "He bragged that he'd own the farm by year's end. He even had the nerve to ask me to stay on as head chef of The Foxhole."

Casey shakes her head in disgust. "Someone needs to make this craziness stop." And that someone might be her. If she develops a relationship with Daniel, perhaps she can convince him to tell Hugh and Charles to back off.

Fiona and Casey enter the Blue Saloon, where a bluegrass band is playing on stage. They pass through to the deck out back and grab two seats at the bar.

The bartender tosses two cocktail napkins in front of them. "What will it be, ladies? The usual?" he asks, and they nod.

"Do you think Larry's cute?" Fiona whispers as he fills two glasses with fizzy champagne.

"I've never thought about it because he's too old." Casey scrutinizes the bartender. "But he has a nice butt. Maybe if he cut his hair."

Larry deposits the champagne in front of them. "Shall we start a tab?" he asks, one corner of his mouth curling into a smile.

"Please!" Fiona says.

Casey's eyes follow Larry as he moves to the other end of the bar. "I have to say his lopsided smile is kinda sexy. Do *you* find him attractive?"

"Not really. I agree he's too old. Like forty or something." Fiona takes a sip of champagne. "When's the last time you had sex?"

Casey is taken aback. It's been a long time since she had girl-friends to discuss such matters. "I can't remember, honestly. Since before Mom got sick. What about you?"

Fiona sighs. "I can't remember either. I don't have an excuse, except that I've been busy building my career."

"I consider that a legitimate excuse."

"Maybe." Fiona plants her elbows on the bar and chin in hand. "I think maybe there's something wrong with me. I haven't found any guy attractive since moving here."

Casey cocks an eyebrow at her. "You just admitted you've been focused on your career. It's Saturday night, and this place is hopping. Surely there's someone here you find cute."

"I highly doubt it," Fiona says. "But it's worth a look."

Turning in their seats, they survey the male occupants on the deck.

"What about him?" Casey asks, her gaze traveling to a lanky guy standing against the railing.

"Too tall. We'd look like Mutt and Jeff."

"What about the cute guy wearing a blue striped shirt over near the door?"

"Nah, he's too short. Our children would be midgets."

Their conversation continues like this until they've dissected every single guy on the deck.

Exasperated, Fiona tosses her hands in the air. "Who am I to judge others by their looks? Besides, it doesn't matter what's on the outside. It's what's in people's hearts that counts."

Casey laughs. "Who are you trying to convince? Me or yourself?"

"Myself, I guess." They turn back around and signal to Larry for a refill. "Have you ever kissed a girl, Casey?"

Casey lets out a nervous laugh. "Um . . . No! Have you?"

"Nope. Have you ever thought about it?" Fiona asks, shredding her napkin.

"Can't say that I have." Casey nudges Fiona with her elbow. "Clearly you have, or we wouldn't be having this conversation."

Before Fiona can respond, the woman seated next to her vacates her barstool, and a cute guy dressed in a gray suit sits down. He orders a draft beer from Larry and smiles over at Fiona. "So, this is where the excitement is."

Fiona sits back in her chair and crosses her legs. "About as much excitement as you'll find in Lovely on a Saturday night."

A wave of dirty-blond hair sweeps over his forehead, and his clear green eyes shine. "I just came from my cousin's wedding reception at Love-Struck vineyards. What a bore. My cheeks hurt from my old lady relatives pinching them. I'm Jack, by the way. In town for the weekend from Richmond."

Fiona accepts his outstretched hand. "I'm Fiona." She flicks a wrist in Casey's direction. "And this is my roommate, Casey. We live here in town."

"What do you do for a living?" Jack asks, his question directed at Fiona.

"I'm head chef at Foxtail Farm, the vineyard two miles down the road from Love-Struck. We just opened The Foxhole, a lunch cafe and soon-to-be tasting room."

Jack nods approvingly. "I'm a chef as well."

Fiona's eyes widen. "Really? Where?"

"At an upscale restaurant in a historic area of Richmond known as Shockoe Slip."

"I've been to Shockoe. That's a charming street."

"Love-Struck needs a new chef. The food at the reception was . . ." Jack sticks a finger in his mouth, as though to gag himself.

Fiona laughs. "That good, huh?"

Casey remembers what Sheldon said about the food at Love-Struck. *Our food isn't even that great.* "How do they stay in business?" Fiona asks.

"Because their focus is on presentation," Jack says. "I give them credit for putting on a spectacular show."

Casey finishes her champagne while Fiona and Jack carry on a private conversation about food. She doesn't mind being left out. Based on their earlier conversation, Fiona is way overdue a crush.

Fiona's and Jack's heads are close together by the time Casey pays her portion of the tab. She tugs on the sleeve of Fiona's jean jacket. "I'm going home now. You two have fun."

Fiona casts her a concerned glance. "Are you okay to walk home alone?"

"I'll be fine. It's not even dark out yet." She kisses Fiona's cheek and leaves the deck.

The sun is setting as she strolls down Magnolia Avenue and over two blocks to the cottage. Changing into her pajamas, she curls up on the sofa with a blanket, a cup of hot tea, and a romance novel. She falls asleep before she finishes the first chapter.

The sun is streaming through the windows when she wakes the next morning at seven thirty. Untangling herself from the blanket, she hurries upstairs to check on Fiona, but her room-mate's bedroom door is open, her bed still made from the previous day.

Casey goes back down to the kitchen and brews herself a cup of coffee. She's sitting at the breakfast counter, scrolling through emails on her phone and wondering how she'll spend her day off, when Fiona arrives home. Casey takes her coffee into the living room. "Well? How was it?"

"I don't want to talk about it," Fiona says, dropping her keys on the table beside the front door.

Casey's eyes narrow. "Did something happen? He seemed like a nice guy?"

"He's a super nice guy. I just don't want to talk about it, okay?"

Fiona's tone warns Casey to back off. "Okay."

"I've gotta get to work," Fiona says, heading for the stairs.

Casey calls up after her, "I'm free all day. I can help at the cafe if you need me."

Fiona pauses at the top of the stairs. "We should be fine. I imagine business will be slow after yesterday. But I'll call you if anything changes," she says and disappears around the corner to her room.

Casey's phone vibrates in her hand. She looks down at the text from Daniel Love. *Are you free for lunch today?*

She waits a few minutes before responding. *Yes.*

Daniel: *How's twelve o'clock? Do you mind coming to my house? I live just past the winery. We can talk in private.*

Casey: *See you then.*

She presses the phone to her chest. This is really happening. She's having lunch with her father.

CHAPTER 6

Impressive stone walls and columns mark the entrance to Daniel's property. Casey follows the paved driveway up a hill and behind Love-Struck Vineyard. A bronze placard on a stone pillar announces her arrival at The Love Nest. She snickers to herself. Who calls a sprawling stone mansion with turrets and arched dormer windows a nest?

The American and Virginia state flags flap in the breeze from tall poles in the center of the circular driveway. Casey parks beside the double front doors and gets out of the car. A housekeeper in a gray uniform dress welcomes her with a grim face and leads her down a wide center hallway to a bluestone terrace.

Daniel, wearing a striped golf shirt and khaki pants, is standing at a knee wall and staring out over the mountains. The spectacular view easily rivals the one at Foxtail Farm. If the older Love brothers are so desperate for land with a view, why not tear down their father's estate and build their resort here?

The housekeeper clears her throat, breaking Daniel's reverie. He crosses the terrace toward them. "So good to see you, my dear," he says and kisses both of Casey's cheeks.

The housekeeper hovers nearby, as though hoping to learn the young visitor's identity. Daniel gives her a curt nod. "That'll be all for now, Beatrice."

He watches Beatrice disappear inside before turning his attention back to Casey. He gives her the once-over. "You're a breath of fresh air."

"Thank you." This is the reaction she was hoping for when she chose the floral sundress instead of her drab brown pantsuit.

"I appreciate you coming on such short notice." He gestures at a small table set for two. "Lunch is ready whenever we want to eat. However, if you have the time, I thought we'd take a walk around the property first."

Casey offers him a soft smile. "I'd like that."

They descend a short flight of steps onto the lawn and stroll down the hill toward a manicured rose garden.

"I haven't been able to get you off my mind since yesterday," Daniel says. "Seeing you has brought back so many memories of the summer I spent with your mother. How much did she tell you about our relationship?"

"Not much. How did you two meet?" Casey prefers to hear his side of the story before telling him what little she knows about his affair with her mother.

"We were renting neighboring cottages in Napa. Your mother was taking a much-needed break from the network, and I a much-needed break from my troubled marriage. I made the mistake of not telling Beverly I was married. I told her I was researching advances in winemaking methods, which was true to a certain extent."

"Why didn't you tell her you were married?"

Daniel pauses a beat before answering. "Beverly made it clear she wasn't looking for a long-term relationship. And my life in Virginia seemed so far away. Lila, my wife, and I had been through some challenging years. I wanted to escape, if only for the summer. Your mom and I fell madly in love. It sounds corny, but I've never felt that way about anyone before or since."

When they reach the rose garden, Daniel steps out of the way to let Casey enter first. The garden is divided into quadrants outlined by neatly trimmed boxwood hedges. In the center is a fountain featuring a bronze statue of a maiden with water spilling from the conch shell balanced on her head.

Casey takes a deep breath, filling her lungs with the sweet scent of roses. "Your home is amazing. I'm curious about the name, The Love Nest."

Daniel smiles. "My great grandfather developed this land in the late eighteen hundreds. Legend has it, he was a bit of a joke-ster. Calling a ten-thousand square foot mansion a nest is a bit of an oxymoron, don't you think? Over the years the family has dropped the Love part, and now we just call it The Nest. Which isn't far off the mark. A nest, or roost, is a place where birds return at the end of the day."

Casey yearns to ask about his little birdies but saves that conversation for later. Lowering herself to a concrete bench, she asks, "When did you finally tell Mom you were married?"

Daniel sits down beside her. "The night before she was to return to New York. Beverly wasn't surprised when I confessed. She'd sensed I was keeping something from her. Being a husband and father made me a safe lover. She could have her summer fling and return to her life with no strings attached."

Casey snickers. "That sounds like Mom."

"I asked Beverly to marry me. I was prepared to divorce my wife. I couldn't let her go, couldn't imagine my life without her. But she insisted the price my family would pay would be too great. And she worried the rumors about her breaking up a marriage would destroy her reputation and ruin her career."

"That also sounds like Mom. So you returned to your wife and children," Casey says.

He presses his lips thin. "I vowed to give my marriage another chance. And I tried. Two months later, Lila found out she was pregnant with my youngest, Ada. But I couldn't get Beverly out of my head. I kept hoping she'd change her mind about me. I watched *The Good Morning Show* every day, foolishly searching for signs that she missed me. I was surprised when she went on another extended leave of absence in December, after she'd been away from the network all summer. But it makes sense now. She took an early maternity leave to hide her pregnancy."

"She protected me by keeping me out of the limelight. Only her closest friends knew she had a daughter. I was her dirty little secret."

Daniel angles his body toward Casey. "I don't believe that for a minute. When Beverly returned to the show the following summer, I could tell she'd changed. She radiated exuberance. I assumed she'd met someone new. Now I know *you* were the one responsible for that newfound happiness. Was she a good mother? Were the two of you close?"

"Yes, and yes." Casey leaves the bench and walks over to the fountain. She picks up a handful of pebbles from the path and tosses them one by one into the water. "Our relationship was unconventional. We were more friends than mother and daughter. She gave me the best of everything, and I always felt loved," she says, her throat thick with unshed tears.

Daniel joins her at the fountain, and they stand together in companionable silence for several minutes. "Was she sick long?"

"Just shy of three years. After the network forced her to retire, she fell into a deep depression. She went weeks without getting out of bed. She let things slide, including her health insurance. The cancer treatments and nursing care ate up all her savings. I had to quit my job to take care of her. After her death, I sold the apartment to cover the hospital bills."

"I'm so sorry, Casey. I'd like to help you out if you need money," Daniel says, his tone sincere.

"I didn't tell you all that to make you feel sorry for me. I thought you should know, since you obviously cared about her." Casey turns to face Daniel. "Thanks for the offer, but I didn't come here for money. Like I said yesterday, I just wanted to meet you."

"Well, I'm glad you're here." He loops his arm through hers. "I don't know about you, but I'm getting hungry."

"Starving," she says, and allows him to escort her back up the hill to the terrace.

He pulls her chair out and waits until she's settled before taking the seat opposite her. He removes a bottle of Veuve Clicquot from the ice bucket next to him and pops the cork. "The occasion calls for a celebration." He fills two seamless flutes, sliding one across the table to her. "Cheers! To Beverly."

With a sad smile, Casey touches her flute to his. "To Mom."

Beatrice delivers the first course. In a huff of irritation, she deposits their salad plates in front of them. Daniel's gaze follows her as she hurries from the terrace. "I apologize for Beatrice's sour mood. She's irritated at having to serve us. Normally, Marabella, our cook, would tend to us. But she has Sundays off."

Casey stares down at her salad—fresh baby spinach with bacon crumbles and grated hard-boiled egg. "This looks delicious. Did Beatrice prepare the meal?"

Daniel appears pleased at the compliment. "Actually, I made it. I'm no gourmet, but I can handle simple dishes."

Casey takes a gulp of champagne, summoning liquid courage to ask him about her siblings. "Tell me about your children."

"Well . . . Hugh and Charles are Irish twins, Hugh being the oldest by eleven months. He's married with two little devils." Daniel chuckles. "Watching them torture him gives me great pleasure."

"I take it Hugh was a mischievous child."

"That's an understatement," Daniel says, attacking his salad. "Charles is also married. His wife is a saint for putting up with his grumpy demeanor. They've been unable to have children, which may be the reason for his foul mood. I wouldn't know. He doesn't share much about his personal life."

"Are Charles and Hugh close? Maybe Charles opens up to Hugh about his problems?"

Daniel grunts. "I doubt it. Charles is reserved by nature. And Hugh is not the touchy feely type." He pours more champagne into their flutes. "You said you've met Sheldon. He's the most like me."

"How so?" Casey asks, peering at him over the rim of her flute as she sips champagne.

"He's more laid back. The others inherited their mother's dark side. You'll meet them eventually. My affair with your mother shouldn't come as a surprise to them. Ours was not a happy home. They were acutely aware of the marital problems. Regardless, I'll need to handle the situation delicately."

Casey's stomach churns, and she sets down her fork. "I don't want to cause any trouble. I understand if you'd prefer to keep our relationship on the down-low."

Daniel wipes his mouth with his napkin. "That is not at all what I want. You're my child, every bit as much as they are. If your mother had told me about her pregnancy, I would have acknowledged you when you were born."

"That means a lot, Daniel. Thank you."

Out of the corner of her eye, Casey notices a shadowy figure looming behind a porch column. She glances away for a split second, and when she looks back, the figure is gone. Perhaps the bright sun is playing tricks on her eyes.

Minutes later, Beatrice bustles out of the house with a tray bearing two domed plates. She removes the salads from the table and places a shallow rimmed bowl of shrimp and grits in front of them.

Casey waits for the housekeeper to leave before sampling the food. "This is amazing. Mom was a gourmet cook. Did you two ever cook together?"

A faraway expression crosses Daniel's face. "All the time."

"Your children will want proof that I'm your child. And I don't blame them."

Daniel jabs his fork at her. "The proof is on your face. Sheldon is my look-alike, and you're a younger, female version of him."

"That's not the same as a DNA test."

"Let me worry about my children. If they choose not to accept you, then that's their problem." Daniel reaches across the table for Casey's hand. "You may have my physical features, but you inherited your ethereal aura from Beverly. That inner light is what attracted me to her. I've always regretted not pursuing Beverly. I should've followed her to New York and begged her to marry me. Through you, God has given me the piece of your mother I cherished the most. Now that I've found you, golden girl, I have no intention of letting you go."

Casey doesn't realize tears are streaming down her cheeks until Daniel hands her his linen handkerchief. "I didn't mean to make you cry."

She accepts the handkerchief and dabs at her eyes. "No one has ever said anything so touching to me." She glances toward the house. "I need to use the restroom."

"Sure." He gestures at the french doors. "Just inside, second door on the right."

Casey fights back more tears as she hurries inside to the powder room. She closes the toilet lid and sits down, gulping in air to steady her breath. Is this really happening? This man is her dream daddy come true. They've only just met, yet she already feels a special connection with him. But she questions whether she can trust him. Fiona called him a hard-ass. Either that's untrue, or the man has an alter ego.

Casey studies her surroundings as she composes herself. A gray-and-white wallpaper in a lattice design covers the walls and an old chest of drawers with a hammered brass sink serves as the washbasin. She's dying to explore the rest of The Nest. Maybe one day she'll get a chance.

She returns to the table, and while they finish their meal, she tells him about her life with Beverly in New York.

After lingering over strawberry shortcake and coffee, Casey pushes back from the table. "I can't remember when I've had such a decadent meal for lunch. But I really should be going. I have Sunday chores to attend to at home."

"Of course. I'll walk you out." They pass through the grand hallway to the driveway.

Daniel opens her car door for her. "I'll be in touch. Sooner rather than later, because I'm very much looking forward to seeing you again. I hate to ask this of you again, but can we keep our relationship between us a little longer? Until I have a chance to speak with each of my children, individually."

Casey drags her fingers across her lips. "I promise not to say a word."

Warmth spreads through her body as she leaves the estate. She was blessed to have her mother for the first twenty-five years of her life. God willing, she'll have her father for the next twenty-five.

CHAPTER 7

Thoughts of Daniel Love creep into Casey's mind at work on Monday morning. She daydreams about him walking her down the aisle at her wedding and reading stories to her children by the fire on Christmas Eve. All the fatherly things Casey has never let herself hope for are now within her reach.

She takes a stroll around the vineyard at lunchtime to clear her head. She's walking back up to the house when her cell rings with a call from Daniel. Her heart races. She wasn't expecting to hear from him so soon.

Daniel blurts, "Word about me being your father has leaked out. Any idea how that happened?" His accusatory tone sets her on edge. So, this is the other side of Daniel Love.

"None. I certainly didn't tell anyone." A memory of the shadowy figure flashes in her mind. "Although I think someone may have been eavesdropping on us while we were having lunch." She tells him about the shadowy figure lurking behind the columns.

"Beatrice! I should've known. My wife hired her. Her allegiance is to . . ." Daniel stops himself. "Never mind. I don't need to air my family's dirty laundry."

His words sting. *His* family's dirty laundry, which Casey is not a part of.

"Sorry to bother you," Daniel says curtly and ends the call, taking Casey's dreams for a close father/daughter relationship with him.

Casey increases her pace as she continues toward the house. Ollie is on the porch, having what appears to be an intense conversation with someone on her cell phone. Casey slips into the kitchen and pours herself a glass of sweet tea. She returns the pitcher to the refrigerator. When she turns around, Ollie is standing in the doorway, glaring at her.

"I can't believe you're Daniel Love's daughter," Ollie says, her mouth twisted with distaste.

"News certainly travels fast around here," Casey says, and braces for the tongue lashing she knows is coming.

"Fast?" Ollie scoffs. "You've been working here nearly two months. I'd say you took your sweet time in sharing that news. Oh, wait! You didn't share it with me. I had to hear it from Sheldon."

Casey goes rigid. "Sheldon knows about this?"

"Forget about Sheldon. How much did you tell Daniel Love about my business?"

Casey bristles at her accusation. "I didn't tell him anything about your business. I only just met him on Saturday."

The front door slams, and Jamie appears in the kitchen. "What's going on? Why all the yelling?"

Ollie sweeps an arm at Casey. "Little Benedict Arnold here has been spying on me. Turns out she's Daniel Love's bastard child, the product of an affair he had years ago."

Anger rises in her chest. "I'm not spying on you, Ollie. I would never do that. I didn't find out who my father was until after my mother died. I wanted to meet him. You would've done the same thing in my shoes."

Ollie plants a hand on her hip. "Maybe. But I wouldn't have used my work situation to get close to him."

Casey stares down at the floor. "I was buying time until I came up with a way to approach him. I couldn't very well knock on his door and introduce myself as the long-lost daughter he never knew about."

Ollie jabs a finger at her. "So you admit it. You used your work situation to get closer to him. You took advantage of me."

Casey looks up at her. "I don't see it that way at all. I needed a job, and you needed a graphic designer."

"You should've told me the truth, Casey."

"I planned to tell you eventually. But I worried how you'd take the news considering how you feel about the Love family."

"All the more reason you should've told me," Ollie snaps.

"Your obsession with the Loves isn't healthy," Casey ventures, borrowing a play out of Jamie's playbook.

"This isn't about me," Ollie says, stabbing her chest with her thumb.

Casey looks at Jamie, hoping he'll back her up. His gaze travels back and forth between Casey and Ollie, apparently conflicted as to whose side to take.

"Whatever." Casey spins on her heels and storms out of the room. Grabbing her purse from the office, she hurries out of the house and races her car down the driveway. Instead of taking a left toward home, she goes right, headed farther away from town.

Voices echo in her mind as she drives aimlessly through the mountains. Daniel, accusing her of leaking the news before abruptly ending their call. Ollie's irate tone. *You used your work situation to get closer to him. You took advantage of me.* Jamie's unwillingness to take Casey's side, despite having frequently expressed his frustration over Ollie's obsession with the Loves. And Sheldon, the one person she thought she could count on. She knew he'd need time to adjust to the idea of her being his half sister. But instead of reaching out to her when he heard the news, he'd gone straight to Ollie. Ollie called Casey *Daniel Love's bastard child, the product of an affair he had years ago.* Was Ollie repeating Sheldon's words?

What a mess. Casey had envisioned herself facilitating peace between Ollie and the Loves. But she's gone and made matters so much worse.

An hour later, she finds herself back at the cottage. She locks herself in her room, crawls into bed, and cries herself to sleep. The warm hues of dusk have fallen over the room when she wakes. She sits up in bed and retrieves her phone from the bedside table. She's disappointed to find no missed calls or text messages from Daniel or Sheldon.

She came to Lovely to meet her father. Now that she's accomplished her mission, she can move on. What's the point in hanging around where she's not wanted? Assuming Ollie will provide a reference, she should be able to find another job. She's saved a little money while working for Ollie, and she still has some of her inheritance left. She'll be fine for a few weeks until she can figure out where she wants to land. Maybe one of the up-and-coming Southern cities like Raleigh or Charlotte or Nashville.

Swinging her legs over the side of the bed, she removes her suitcase from the closet and begins packing the contents of her chest of drawers.

She hears the front door slam, followed by footfalls on the stairs. "What're you doing?" Fiona asks from the doorway.

"I'm packing. I assume you heard what happened. I'm sorry to abandon you, but I can't stay here."

Fiona enters the room. "I heard. I don't know why Ollie is being such a bitch. I think it's seriously cool that Daniel Love is your biological father. I wish you'd told me, but I understand why you didn't. Please don't go, Casey. I don't know what I'll do without you," she says and bursts into tears.

"Hey." Casey drops an armload of bras and panties into her suitcase and takes Fiona in her arms. "What's wrong, Fi? You haven't been yourself since you hooked up with Jack on Saturday night. Does this have something to do with him?"

"Yes, and no." Fiona pulls away. "I need to talk to you about something. Will you at least stay one more night?"

Casey hands Fiona a tissue from the box on her nightstand. "Sure. I wasn't planning to leave until tomorrow anyway." She motions Fiona to the bed. "Shall we sit down?"

Fiona shakes her head. "I need liquid courage. I have a bottle of red wine in the kitchen. I'll grab it and meet you in the living room," she says and hurries down the stairs.

Casey transfers the rest of her underwear to her suitcase, zips it up, and places it on the floor beside the bed. Fiona is pouring red wine into two glasses when she joins her on the sofa in the living room.

"This will be easier for me to say in the dark," Fiona says, turning off the lamp beside the sofa.

"You're scaring me, Fiona. What's wrong? Please tell me Jack didn't rape you."

Fiona guzzles some wine and licks her lips. "It's nothing like that. Jack was a true gentleman. It's just that . . ." She takes a deep breath. "I'm in love with you, Casey."

A golden eyebrow rises. "Since when are you gay?"

"Since I met you," Fiona says, her voice barely audible.

Casey thinks back to their conversation at the Blue Moon. "So that's why you asked if I'd ever thought about kissing a girl?"

The dim light from the porch lamp shines through the window, illuminating Fiona's anguished face. "Yep." She falls back against the cushions. "I've had plenty of boyfriends in the past, but none of them have ever truly lit my fire. I couldn't stop thinking about you the other night when I was making out with Jack. I explained my confusion to him, and we talked for hours. He's a good guy. Very understanding. He encouraged me to explore these feelings."

"I don't know what to say, Fi. I love you. As a friend. Romance in any form is the last thing on my mind right now."

Fiona's eyes glisten with tears. "I figured you'd say that." She cracks a smile. "But I had to at least try."

Casey sips her wine as she ponders Fiona's confession. "Jack is right. You should explore these feelings with someone who can return them."

"I seriously don't think I'm gay. Or bisexual. Or whatever. I'm just attracted to you. You're drop-dead gorgeous, and you have a super sweet personality. Any man or woman would be lucky to have you as their partner."

"Just not as their daughter or sister," Casey says under her breath. "It's a good thing I'm leaving. You can all move on with your lives."

"You can't go! Even if you don't return my feelings, I need you here to sort out my sexual identity crisis. You're the best friend I've had in years."

"I have to work, Fi, and I'm pretty sure I no longer have a job."

"I saw Ollie this afternoon. She'd calmed down a lot. She actually seemed remorseful."

Casey checks her phone. "She hasn't called, so she must not be too remorseful. After the way she behaved today, I'm not sure I want to work for her any longer. I'm not perfect, and I said some things I shouldn't have, but I'm beginning to think Ollie has an anger management problem."

"No question about it. But enough about me and Ollie. I still can't believe Daniel Love is your father. Start at the beginning and tell me everything."

CHAPTER 8

Loud banging on the door wakes Casey from a deep slumber around seven thirty on Tuesday morning. Throwing her robe on over her shorty pajamas, she hurries down the stairs in bare feet. Swinging open the door, she's surprised to find Sheldon on the front porch holding two coffees.

Sheldon's jaw drops when he sees her. "Wow! Your hair looks like mine in the morning."

"What're you doing here?" she asks, gathering her messy waves into a ponytail and securing it with an elastic from her wrist.

"I was worried about you. I wanted to catch you before you went to work."

"I'm not going in today. I'm not even sure I still have a job."

He narrows his eyes. "Ollie hasn't contacted you?"

"Not unless she texted during the night." Casey gestures at the stairs. "My phone's in my room."

Sheldon hands her a coffee. "Cream only, the way you like it."

"Thanks," she says, and takes a tentative sip.

"Can we talk for a minute?"

"I guess." She ties her robe tighter and follows him across the porch to the bench swing.

"I'm sorry for the way everything went down yesterday," Sheldon says. "When I heard the rumor, I called Ollie to find out if she knew anything. I didn't mean to set her off."

"I thought we were friends, Sheldon. Why didn't you come to me instead of reaching out to Ollie?"

"Because I, too, thought we were friends. And I felt betrayed. Why didn't you tell me the truth?"

"I came to Lovely with the sole purpose of finding my biological father. But I wasn't sure how to approach him. When Ollie offered me a job, I put meeting him on the back burner while I settled into my life. Then I ran into him at the grand opening. He recognized the resemblance. When he asked my name, I confessed that my mother was Beverly Hobbs. He put two and two together. I didn't mean for anyone to get hurt. Most especially you. My mother kept him from me all these years because she didn't want to disrupt your family. And that's exactly what's happened. I should never have come here."

"Despite what anyone else thinks, I'm glad you're here." He rests an arm on the swing behind her. "I can't believe you're my little sister. I knew something was different about you. I felt a connection with you, but I wasn't attracted to you. Which is weird because you're so damn beautiful." He chuckles. "That's an arrogant thing to say, considering you're a female version of me."

Casey touches a finger to his cleft chin. "It's uncanny, isn't it? Like one of those apps where you switch faces with another person. You're the spitting image of your dad."

"He's *our* dad, Casey."

"That will take some getting used to." She lowers her hand. "I feel awful. I didn't mean to cause so much trouble for Daniel."

Sheldon barks out a laugh. "Trouble? You started World War Three. We've always been a divided family. Until now, it's been my siblings versus Dad and me. Now we have you to even the playing field."

Tears pool in her eyes. "Is that's supposed to make me feel

better? Because it doesn't. It only reinforces my decision to leave town."

"What're you talking about?" Sheldon says, adjusting his body so he can see her. "You can't leave now."

Casey shrugs. "I've already packed my suitcase."

"But we just discovered you. You'll break Dad's heart."

"I doubt that," she says with a sniffle.

"Seriously, Casey." Sheldon cups her cheeks and thumbs away her tears. "I've never seen Dad like this before. I had dinner with him last night. He told me all about your mother. He obviously loved her very much. My parents were miserable in their marriage. I'm glad to know he had some happiness, even if it was only for a brief three months. You make him happy, Casey. His face lights up when he talks about you."

"Then why hasn't he called?"

"Dad is not one to make rash decisions. He has a lot to figure out. He wants to be fair to everyone involved."

Sheldon's words calm her. This is what Casey expects of a father—to be fair to all his children, including the illegitimate ones.

Sheldon jumps up suddenly and pulls Casey to her feet. "I'm starving. Let me buy you breakfast at Ruthie's, and we can talk more about all this."

Prying her hands free, Casey plops back down. "I can't. I have a long drive ahead of me."

"Then you should eat before you get on the highway," he says, pulling her up again.

Casey smiles at his tenacity. "You're not taking no for an answer, are you?"

He laughs. "Nope."

"All right." Casey glances down at her bathrobe. "Let me get dressed. I'll be right back."

She hurries up to her room to change. When she comes back downstairs, Sheldon is waiting for her in his car.

Ruthie's is crowded, but there are two seats available at the counter. Feeling inquiring eyes on her, Casey hides behind the menu. "This was a bad idea. I feel like I'm the star of the freak show at the state fair."

"Stop it!" Sheldon snatches the menu from her. "If they're staring at you, it's because you're so angelic."

Ruthie appears in front of them, and they both order the breakfast burrito special with sides of hash browns. If Ruthie has heard the news, she doesn't let on. She fills their mugs with coffee before hurrying off to place their order.

"Do you have another job lined up somewhere?" Sheldon asks, dumping a packet of sweetener in his coffee.

"No, I'm thinking I'll try Charlotte first. If I can't find anything there, I'll move on to Nashville."

"I can't imagine what it was like for you growing up without a father. Now that you have a chance to know him, why would you run off?" Sheldon asks, a mischievous glint in his eyes despite his somber tone.

"I already told you. I don't want to cause trouble for your family."

"Change is never easy, Casey. But sometimes it's good to mix things up. I think you're just the change my family needs right now."

"How so?" Casey asks, peering at him over the rim of her mug.

"Because my siblings abuse their positions in the company. They do whatever they want with total disregard for how their decisions impact others. A blast from Dad's past is just what we need to shake things up, to make them stop taking their wealth and privilege for granted."

"Great," Casey says, rolling her eyes. "So now I'm a blast from your dad's past."

Ruthie delivers their plates and Sheldon digs into his breakfast burrito. "Won't you give it a little more time, Casey? For my sake and for Dad's."

Squirting ketchup on her hash browns, Casey says, "I think

you're wrong about Daniel. If he cares so much, he would've called."

"He sent me to see you instead."

"What?" Casey freezes, a forkful of hash browns near her lips. "But I thought—"

Sheldon's hand flies up, silencing her. "I would've come on my own anyway. He's worried about you. He wanted me to make sure you're okay. You can't leave town, Casey. Not yet anyway."

Casey touches her phone screen to check for texts. She was due at work thirty minutes ago, yet Ollie hasn't bothered to call to see if she overslept or was involved in a car accident. "I can't stay if I don't have a job."

"I'm sure we can find something for you at Love-Struck."

"No way! That would be the nuclear bomb that destroys your family."

Her phone pings with a text from Ollie. *Are you coming in today?*

Sheldon reads the text. "See! I told you. You still have a job."

Picking up the phone, Casey swivels on the stool so Sheldon can't see her response. *Wasn't planning on it.*

Ollie responds, *At least come out to the farm so we can talk.*

Casey hesitates. What does she have to lose? If nothing else, she can ask Ollie for a reference. She thumbs off her reply. *Be there soon.*

When she looks up from her phone, Sheldon is staring at her. "Well?"

"I'll talk to her, but after the things she said yesterday, I'm not sure I can work there anymore."

"You shouldn't be so hard on Ollie," Sheldon says, chomping into a buttermilk biscuit.

Casey cuts her eyes at him. "Why are you defending her?"

"Because she's not herself right now."

Casey softens, remembering Ollie's parents' recent deaths. "You're right. Losing my mother is the worst thing that's ever happened to me. I can't imagine what it's like having both parents die at the same time."

"Imagine if your brother was serving two life sentences for killing them."

Casey gives her head a vigorous shake. Surely she heard him wrong. "What did you just say?"

"Ollie's brother started the fire that killed her parents."

Casey clamps her hand over her mouth. "Oh my god. That's the worst thing I've ever heard."

"Ollie is on top of her game with her business. But personally, her head's a mess. But when her mind clears, and she realizes Jamie is all wrong for her, I'll be waiting in the wings. And so will you."

"What's that supposed to mean?"

"You know what that means. You're as hung up on Jamie as I am on Ollie."

Casey's face warms. "Is it that obvious?"

"Only to me," Sheldon says, but Casey suspects he's lying. Does everyone know she has a crush on Jamie? More importantly, does Jamie know she has a crush on him?

CHAPTER 9

Ollie is seated on a barstool, drumming her fingers on the kitchen counter, when Casey arrives at the farm.

Casey drops her bag on the seat next to Ollie. "Sorry. I was having breakfast with Sheldon."

Annoyance flashes in Ollie's eyes, and when she opens her mouth to speak, Casey prepares for another tirade. Instead, Ollie surprises her with an apology.

"I'm sorry about yesterday. I don't have any reason to question your loyalty . . . Do I?"

"You have no reason to question my loyalty." Casey leans against the counter, folding her arms over her chest. "Daniel and I have more to talk about than my job at Foxtail Farm."

Ollie sips from her coffee mug. "Because you've only just met. But after a while, he'll start pumping you for information. Your allegiance may change, now that you're one of them."

"I'm not one of anybody. I answer only to myself." Casey walks over to the open doorway and stares out across the vineyard. She's grown accustomed to this view. She likes her job. But something has shifted in her relationship with Ollie. Casey can't work for someone who doesn't trust her.

With her back to Ollie, Casey says, "Clearly, you're uncomfortable with this situation. I think it's best if I hand in my resignation."

Ollie comes to stand beside her. "That's not what I want, Casey. You're extremely talented, a true asset to my team. I believe we can work through this if we're both willing to try."

Casey chews on her lip as she considers the situation. Can she really leave town with so many things unsettled? She'll always wonder what might have been with Daniel. With Sheldon. With Jamie. She needs a little more time. She remembers what Sheldon said about Ollie. *Imagine if your brother was serving two life sentences for killing them.* Why not give her another chance?

Casey turns toward Ollie. "We're set to launch the marketing campaign in two weeks. I'd like to see this project through. Why don't we reassess the situation then?"

"That sounds like a reasonable plan." Ollie grabs her straw hat from the wall hook and slips it on her head. "I'd better get to work."

Casey watches her boss stroll down the driveway and disappear behind the barn. Retrieving a bottled water from the refrigerator, she goes to the office and sits down at her desk. She immerses herself in her work until Sheldon calls around three o'clock.

He sounds out of breath. "Where are you?"

"At work, why?"

"I called to warn you. I overheard my brothers and sister talking. They want you gone, Casey. Be careful. They're a nasty bunch."

Casey pushes away from the desk and rests her head against the back of the chair. "Ollie and I agreed I'd stay until after we launch the marketing campaign. Tell your siblings to back off. In two weeks, I'll be gone."

"So you're just going to run away with your tail between your legs? If you weren't my Mini-Me, I'd question whether we are related. The Loves are fighters. We never give up. You can't let these people bully you. Stand up to them."

Casey closes her eyes, forcing herself to remain calm. "We may look alike, Sheldon, but you and I are cut from different cloth. My mom was the only family I've ever known. No grandparents or cousins or brothers and sisters. I came here to meet my biological father. Not to stir up a hornet's nest of angry siblings."

"You've been deprived of a father all your life, Casey. You deserve to *know* him. And Dad wants that too. Don't let my siblings ruin this for you."

The last thing she wants is to get tangled up with siblings who despise one another. The sooner she can finish this campaign, the sooner she can get the heck out of Dodge. "Thanks for the warning, Sheldon. I'll talk to you later."

Casey slams the phone down on her desk and returns her attention to her computer. By the time she looks up again, daylight has faded and darkness is setting in. Her stomach rumbles. She hasn't eaten since breakfast. She calls Fiona to see if she wants to grab dinner, but her roommate doesn't answer.

Casey hears Ollie stirring around in the kitchen, but she doesn't stop to speak to her on her way out. No lights are on in the cottage, and Fiona's car isn't in the driveway. She doesn't notice the figure on the swing until she mounts the porch steps. When Ada gets to her feet, Casey jumps back, startled.

"Geez, Ada. You scared me to death," she says, her hand over her racing heart.

Ada shines her phone's flashlight in Casey's face, blinding her. "I don't see the resemblance."

"Get that thing out of my face," Casey says, swatting at the phone.

Ada turns off the flashlight and pockets the phone. "What game are you playing? If it's money you're after, you won't get any."

"I want nothing from you or your family."

"I find that hard to believe." Ada steps close enough for Casey to smell her musky perfume. "I want you gone."

Casey inches toward the door. "Don't worry. I'm leaving in two weeks as soon as I fulfill an obligation at work."

"That's not soon enough. Pack up your stuff and go. Now. Tomorrow at the latest."

"Or else what?" Casey asks, reaching for the doorknob.

Ada glares at her. "Or else I'll make your life miserable."

Casey enters the house, closing and locking the door behind her. She waits until she hears the Mercedes drive off before going to the kitchen. Removing a bottle of chilled rosé from the refrigerator, she pops the cork and takes the bottle and a stemless glass into the living room.

You can't let these people bully you. Stand up to them. Casey is not a fighter. She's out of her league. She knows nothing about family warfare. Best for her to lay low while she's finishing the marketing campaign.

Casey is finishing her second glass of wine when Fiona arrives home. "Where have you been? I've been worried about you," Casey says.

"I went to Hope Springs to see my friends at the inn." She sinks down in the overstuffed chair beside the sofa. "I asked Cecily for my old job back."

"Why would you do such a thing? That's not even a lateral move. It's a demotion."

"The Inn at Hope Springs has become a popular wedding destination. And I was in charge of catering. I don't consider that a demotion." Fiona lets out a sigh. "But that's beside the point. Cecily convinced me to stick it out here for at least a year."

"Why are you suddenly so down on Lovely? I thought you enjoyed living here."

Fiona lowers her gaze to her lap. "The problem isn't the town. The problem is you. I've tried. But I can't shut off my feelings for you."

"I'm sorry, Fiona. I wish I'd never come here. I've wreaked havoc on everyone's lives," Casey says, pouring more wine into her glass.

"Not on mine. You're the best friend I've ever had. Besides, Cecily doesn't think I'm gay. She thinks I have a girl crush." Fiona shrugs. "Maybe she's right. She's setting me up with one of her boyfriend's friends next weekend. I've met Will before. He's not attractive, but he has a cute personality. At least we'll have a good time."

Casey's lips curl into a smile. "You never know. Keep an open mind."

Fiona picks up the wine bottle and studies the label. "What's up with you? Why are you guzzling cheap rosé alone?"

Casey tells Fiona about the warning call from Sheldon and her confrontation with Ada.

"I can't believe she threatened you," Fiona says. "Did you tell Sheldon?"

Casey hangs her head. "What's the point? I'm leaving town as soon as I launch the marketing campaign."

Fiona moves to the edge of her seat. "You're being ridiculous." She jumps to her feet. "I'm going to fix dinner. Are you hungry?"

"Starving, I haven't eaten in hours." Casey stands, loses her footing, and falls back onto the sofa. "Oops."

"We need to get some food in you." Fiona pulls her up, and placing an arm around Casey's waist, she walks her to the kitchen.

"Why do you think I'm being ridiculous? Because I didn't run to Sheldon when Ada threatened me?" Casey asks, chugging a glass of water while Fiona dredges strips of chicken breasts in flour.

Fiona adds a slab of butter to the skillet and watches it melt. "Daniel Love is worth billions. I think you're crazy for walking away from the fairytale lifestyle he can provide."

"I don't want his money," Casey says in a deadpan tone. She sags against the counter. "But I was hoping to have a meaningful relationship with Daniel."

Fiona adds the chicken strips to the skillet and looks up at Casey. "Then why are you giving up so easily?"

"Because I'm no match for Ada Love. And Hugh and Charles. Look what they've done to Ollie."

"You underestimate yourself, Casey. You're Daniel's child, too. You should be a part of his life, and he yours."

"But I have no clue how to handle Ada."

"That's easy." Fiona's lips part in a malicious grin. "You take what's rightfully yours, the one thing Ada doesn't want you to have. Your father."

CHAPTER 10

Casey dreams she loses her job and becomes a homeless bum, living on the streets of New York. When she wakes in a cold sweat on Wednesday morning, the soft rays of dawn are streaming through her blinds. Her head throbs from last night's wine, and when she sits up, the room spins.

Casey needs fresh air to clear her head. Throwing on athletic clothes, she tiptoes down the stairs so as not to wake Fiona. Emerging from the house, she stops dead in her tracks on the edge of the porch at the sight of her car's four flat tires.

Casey stomps the wooden floor. "Damn it!" She pulls out her phone and accesses the Internet. The average price of high-performance tires for a Volvo sedan is four hundred dollars apiece. The expense would put a major dent in her savings account, the money she'd planned to use to start a new life somewhere else.

She clicks on Sheldon's number. He answers on the third ring in a hoarse voice. "This can't be good, if you're calling at the crack of dawn."

"Ada slashed my tires, all four of them."

"Why are you so sure it was Ada?" he asks in a defensive tone, the frog now gone from his throat.

"Because she paid me a visit last night. She threatened to make my life miserable if I don't leave town immediately." Casey sinks to the porch steps. "I grew up in New York, Sheldon. I've never owned a car. The Volvo belonged to my mother. How does one go about getting tires replaced?"

"That's what big brothers are for. Let me put on some clothes. I'll be there in a few minutes."

Fifteen minutes later, Casey is still sitting on the porch steps staring at her flat tires when Sheldon arrives in his Range Rover. She jumps to her feet when a sheriff's patrol car pulls to the curb behind him.

Sheldon gets out of his SUV and goes to greet the uniformed deputy. They shake hands as though they know each other and approach the porch together.

The deputy, who introduces himself as Alfred Kline, scrutinizes her face. "Well, I'll be darn. I didn't believe the rumors. But you can't deny the resemblance. You're the spitting image of your daddy."

Thrusting out his chest, Sheldon adds, "And brother."

"I appreciate you coming, Deputy," Casey says. "But is it necessary to involve the police?"

Kline waves his iPad. "It's always a good idea to file a report. You'll have the documentation in case there's more trouble down the road."

Sheldon places a comforting hand on Casey's back. "And don't forget to tell the deputy about Ada's threat."

"If you're sure." As she tells Kline about last night's visit from Ada and the discovery of her flat tires, Casey has a sinking feeling things will get worse before they get better.

Kline walks the length of the porch, surveying the ceiling and eaves. "I take it you don't have surveillance cameras?"

"No, sir. This is a rental house."

Stepping down from the porch, Kline snaps photographs of the tires with his phone. "Call me if you have any concerns or receive any more threats," he says, handing her his business card.

"Are you going to question Ada?" Sheldon asks.

The deputy tucks his iPad under his arm and adjusts his hat on his head. "There's only so much I can do with no video evidence. But I'll drop by Love-Struck later today and have a little chat with her."

Sheldon and Casey watch the deputy lumber down the side-walk to his patrol car. "I've called a tow truck. It should be here soon. There's a tire dealership over in Hope Springs. The owner is a friend."

Casey doesn't let herself think about how much the tow truck will cost. "Give him my contact info. I'll need to compare prices to get the best deal on tires."

"We'll figure it out," Sheldon says as the tow truck pulls to the curb in front of the cottage. "Can I give you a lift to work?"

"No, but thanks. Fiona's still here. I'll ride in with her."

Casey watches the driver load her mother's Volvo onto the bed of the truck before going inside to shower and dress.

Focusing on work proves to be a challenge during the long morning hours. How could Ada do something so malicious? Fiona is right. If Casey doesn't stand up to her, Ada will continue to push her around. *You take what's rightfully yours, the one thing Ada doesn't want you to have. Your father.*

Casey is eating a salad in the kitchen around noon when a horn blasts in the driveway out front. When she peers through the dining-room window, Sheldon wiggles his fingers at her from behind the steering wheel of her mother's Volvo.

Dumping the remnants of her salad in the trash, she hurries outside. "I told you I wanted to compare prices. Please tell me you didn't pick the most expensive tires."

A devilish smile spreads across his lips. "Oh, I picked the most expensive, all right. But don't worry about it. I took care of it."

"But—"

He presses his finger against his lips. "Shh! I put it on Ada's credit card."

Casey can't help but laugh. "How do you even have her card number?"

"I got it from the file in the office." He hands Casey the car keys. "I need a favor, though. I left my Range Rover at Love-Struck. Do you mind giving me a ride?"

Casey scrunches up her face in confusion. "How'd you get to Hope Springs to pick up the Volvo?"

"I ordered an Uber from Hope Springs. The round trip fare was costly. But I put that charge on Ada's card too."

Opening her car door, Casey says, "Remind me never to get on your bad side."

On the short drive to Love-Struck, Sheldon grows serious. "Ada has taken matters too far. I can't believe she slashed your tires, that she's capable of such a villainous act. Dad needs to know about this, Casey. Do you want to tell him, or should I?"

Casey takes her eyes off the road to look at him. "I'm not a tattletale, Sheldon."

"Dad won't think that of you. I could tell him, but it would mean more coming from you."

She takes a left and passes through the Love-Struck columns. "I don't see why he has to know. You handled the situation. Ada will get what's coming to her when she receives her credit card statement."

His face darkens. "I disagree. But I'll let you have your way for now. If it happens again, we will tell Dad together."

They ride the rest of the way up the driveway in silence. Instead of looking for an empty space in the full parking lot, she pulls in front of the winery and takes the car out of gear.

Sheldon groans when his brother emerges from a small building behind the winery, which Casey assumes is an administrative office. She can't be sure, but she thinks it's Hugh, the same brother who attended The Foxhole opening with Daniel.

The brother strides over to the car and raps on the passenger window. Sheldon rolls down the window. "What do you want, Hugh?"

"Dude, you finally got yourself a girlfriend." Hugh sticks his head in the window to get a better look at the driver. He frowns when he sees Casey. "Oh. It's you." He smacks Sheldon hard on the shoulder. "You may have won over my brother here, but the rest of us want nothing to do with you. I'll kindly ask you to leave my property."

Out of the corner of his mouth, Sheldon says to Casey, "You should leave. You don't want to witness this."

Sheldon swings open the car door. Hugh takes off at a sprint, but he's no match for Sheldon's long stride. Catching up to his brother, Sheldon dives on top and tackles him to the ground.

Casey throws the car into gear and steps on the gas pedal, peeling off out of the parking lot. Her adrenaline skyrockets as she flies down the driveway. The Love brothers are fighting over her. She brought this animosity on this family. The sooner she can get out of town, the better.

She arrives back at Foxtail to find Jamie's SUV parked in front of the farmhouse and him sitting alone on the porch, looking like he lost his best friend. She puts the kettle on for tea and stands in the open doorway. "Are you waiting for Ollie?"

He shifts in the wicker rocker to face her. "I am. Do you know where she is? We were supposed to meet for lunch an hour ago."

Casey shakes her head. "Sorry. I haven't seen her all day. Her Bronco was gone when I arrived this morning."

Jamie slowly rises from his chair. "I'm not surprised. Ollie hasn't been the same since you came out of the closet."

Casey's heart rate quickens. "What do you mean, *out of the closet*?" Does he know Fiona claims to be in love with her?

"Since you announced you're Daniel Love's daughter." Jamie lets out an anguished sigh. "Ollie's preoccupation with the Loves is grating on my nerves. And you consorting with the enemy isn't helping anything."

"I'm not consorting with the enemy, Jamie. Geez!"

Their heads swivel in unison when Ollie's Bronco comes zooming down the driveway and screeches to a halt beside the porch. Ollie climbs out and opens the tailgate. Chard and Rosé bound out of the Bronco and onto the porch. Jamie drops to his knees, cooing to them while they cover his face in licks.

Ollie follows the dogs onto the porch. "I'm sorry about lunch, Jamie. I totally forgot to put it on my calendar. The trainer called. He wanted me to pick up the dogs today. You won't believe what they can do."

Casey slips back into the kitchen. She pours boiling water over a lavender tea bag and retreats to her office, where she remains for the rest of the afternoon.

She's getting in her car around six o'clock when Fiona pulls up next to her. She rolls down the passenger window. "Do you have plans for dinner?"

Casey tosses her bag into the car and walks over to Fiona. "No. What did you have in mind?"

"Belmonte's has a new tasting menu. The chef invited me to sample it. He told me to bring a friend. Wanna come with me?"

"Are you kidding? I could totally gorge on rich Italian food right now."

"Cool! I'm going home to change. I'll meet you there," Fiona says and drives off.

Casey returns to her car and follows Fiona back to the cottage. Upon arrival, they discover the front door ajar. Fiona prods the door open with her shoe, and the roommates stare aghast at the ransacked living room—overturned furniture, broken lamps, contents of the bookshelves littering the floors.

"Who would do this?" Fiona asks, looking at her reflection through the shattered glass of her favorite oyster rimmed mirror.

Casey forces herself to appear calm despite the anger brewing inside. "Ada Love did this. I'm so sorry, Fiona. This is all my fault."

"What should we do?" Fiona asks with tears in her eyes.

"First, we're going to determine if anything was stolen. Then I'll call Deputy Kline and file a report while you go to the tasting."

Fiona swipes at her eyes. "No way! I'm not leaving you with this mess."

"Yes, you are." Casey takes her by the arm and walks her to the stairs. "Now, go change while I look around down here. Be sure to check for anything missing in your room."

Fury explodes inside of Casey as she watches her roommate drag her slumped body up the stairs. Attacking Casey is one thing. But Fiona is an innocent victim. This is the final straw. Ada Love must pay. Game on.

She rights an overturned chair on the way through the living room to the kitchen. Kicking through the trash strewn across the floor, she sits down at the breakfast counter with her phone. After reporting the break-in to Deputy Kline, she places a call to Daniel Love. He answers on the second ring. "Casey, how wonderful to hear from you."

"We need to talk."

"Name the time and place," Daniel says, his tone now serious.

"Eight o'clock tomorrow morning at Ruthie's Diner." Casey ends the call without waiting for him to respond.

CHAPTER 11

Casey arrives at Ruthie's Diner ten minutes early and finds Daniel already seated at a booth in the center of the room where they will be visible to everyone. Holding her head high, she crosses the diner and sits in the booth opposite him.

They've only just exchanged greetings when Ruthie bustles over, a fresh pot of coffee in hand. With a sexy smile on her lips and a flirty tone in her voice, she recites the breakfast specials to Daniel, barely acknowledging Casey's presence. Casey doesn't blame her. He's a handsome man. And Ruthie's a striking woman. They'd make a good-looking couple.

Ruthie hurries away to place their order—egg white omelet for Daniel and oatmeal with fresh berries for Casey.

"You look pretty this morning," Daniel says, his smile soft and tone genuine.

Casey, to let her father know she meant business, had chosen a black sleeveless blouse over gray chinos and pulled her hair back in a tight knot. "This isn't a social call, Daniel. I came to warn you I've petitioned for a restraining order against Ada. Night before last, she slashed all four of my tires. And yesterday while I was at work, she vandalized my home."

Other than a tightening of facial muscles, Daniel remains composed. "Was there much damage to your home?"

"A fair amount. Most of the furnishings belong to my roommate."

Daniel stirs cream into his coffee and takes a sip. "I'll take the money out of Ada's paycheck to reimburse both of you. Get me the receipt for the tires and have Fiona give me a generous estimate of the damages."

Casey smiles, impressed he remembered her roommate's name. "That's kind of you. I'll tell Fiona. But Sheldon already took care of the tires."

Daniel's head jerks back. "Sheldon knows about this?"

"The tires. Not the break-in. He wanted to tell you. But I talked him out of it."

Their food arrives, and they eat for a minute in silence. "I don't blame you for filing for a restraining order. If you feel unsafe, I can provide private security for you. Better yet, you can come live with me at The Nest."

Casey snorts coffee up her nose. "I'm sure that would go over well with Ada," she says, reaching for a napkin.

"I don't care what Ada thinks. Besides, I have an absurd number of guest rooms. You can have your own wing."

Casey studies his face. His earnest expression tells her he's given this considerable thought. "You're serious. When you didn't call, I thought you wanted nothing more to do with me."

Daniel gives his head a solemn shake. "On the contrary. I wanted you to be the one to come to me. I suspected my children would be up to their usual tricks, and I wanted you to understand what you're getting into with my family. I can protect you, but it has to be on your terms."

"That's incredibly thoughtful, Daniel. But I doubt me living at The Nest will stop Ada. What if she comes after me at work? I'd hate to put Ollie in the middle of our . . ." Casey waves her spoon around. "Whatever this is."

"Our family drama." Daniel butters a slice of wheat toast and takes a bite. "You could work remotely."

"I'm not sure Ollie would go for that."

"At least consider the arrangement. Even if it's temporary. Until things settle down. It would give us a chance to get to know each other better."

"I'd like that. It wouldn't be for long. I'm working on a project for Ollie. After we launch the marketing campaign in two weeks, I'm planning to move to a city with better career opportunities." Tears blur Casey's vision as she stares down at her oatmeal. Why is she suddenly so emotional? Is it the thought of leaving her father when she only just found him?

Daniel appears alarmed. "I hate to hear that when we're just getting to know each other." His pale green eyes twinkle with amusement. "I consider it my duty to change your mind. Even more reason for you to stay with me."

"I'll think about it," Casey says, and while she finishes her oatmeal, she imagines herself living at The Nest. Ada would be furious. And isn't that what Casey wants? A victory in the battle over their father. *No!* screams a voice from inside her head. She'd prefer her new family welcome her with open arms.

"Let's get out of here," Daniel says, already on his feet.

Casey grabs her bag and hurries after him. "Wait! We have to pay the check."

"I eat here several times a week. It's easier to keep a running tab and settle up at the end of the month." Daniel holds open the door for her. "Do you have time for a short walk?"

She glances at her watch. "I can spare a few minutes."

They stroll up Magnolia Avenue to the town park and sit down on a bench beside the cement pond, where three little boys wade in the water, pushing plastic boats around amid a cacophony of vrooms.

"I've never admitted this to anyone," Daniel says, his eyes on the boys. "But my children, except for Sheldon, are the greatest disappointment in my life. Their mother spoiled them. She refused to discipline them, and when I tried, she undermined my efforts. They're self-centered egomaniacs, ruthless in their determination to get what they want."

This seems like a harsh thing to say about one's children. Casey thought parents were supposed to love their kids regardless of their actions. "You mentioned their mother had a dark side. Maybe some of it is genetics."

"I'm sure some of it is." Daniel crosses his legs, angling his body toward Casey. "If Ada forces me to choose between you and her, I'll choose you. For twenty-seven years, I've been her father, and you've been without a father. She takes me for granted. I am merely a source of money to her, nothing else."

Casey doesn't know how to respond. She suspects what he says about Ada is true.

"I've felt empty inside since I left your mother in California," Daniel says. "I've thought about it a lot, and I think that emptiness is about more than losing Beverly. I think maybe my soul sensed your presence and ached to be with you. I know it sounds silly. I'm not a mushy type of person. Except when it came to your mother. And now you. I'm not letting you go, Casey. I can't."

Casey's eyes well with tears, and she doesn't trust herself to speak.

"Talking to you is like talking to Beverly, and I know I can trust you to keep this conversation between us. She was the type of person people felt comfortable confiding in. She was a keen listener. She knew how to prod someone into telling her more about themselves."

Swiping at her eyes, Casey says, "She got paid the big bucks to coerce the rich and famous into confessing their darkest secrets on national television."

He rests an arm on the bench behind her. "I know you miss her, sweetheart."

Casey nods. "Very much. Every single day." *But now I've been given a chance to know my father, and I won't let Ada ruin it.* "If you really mean it, I'd like to stay with you until I figure out my life."

"Outstanding!" Daniel jumps up and pulls Casey to her feet. "I'll help you move. Let's go get your stuff."

Casey lets out a girlish giggle. "Not so fast. I have to work today."

"Then text me this afternoon when you leave Foxtail, and I'll meet you at your house."

"That's unnecessary, Daniel. I can handle it on my own."

"I insist. I'll have my staff prepare my favorite suite of rooms for you. There's an adjacent study, which will provide privacy for you to work." She loops her arms through his, and they walk back through town toward the diner. "I'll help you set up your office. I have a supply closet full of monitors and computers."

"I'm not so sure Ollie will agree to me working remotely."

"Why should it matter where you work as long as you're productive?"

Casey debates how much to tell him. "She wasn't thrilled when she found out I'm your daughter."

Daniel stops in his tracks. "What business is it of hers?"

His bewildered expression baffles her. "You seriously don't know?"

"Know what? What're you talking about?"

"You should ask Sheldon. He knows more about the situation than me." Casey lets go of his arm and starts walking again.

He catches up with her in front of the diner. "I'd rather hear it from you. Tell me what she has against me."

"I don't have time right now. I need to get to work," Casey says, clicking her car doors unlocked.

"Then tell me over dinner." Daniel kisses her cheek. Over his shoulder, Casey spots Ada's Mercedes parked on the curb on the next block over. Ada glares at her through the windshield, and Casey wiggles her fingers in response.

Casey gets in her car, starts the engine, and rolls down the window. "Thanks for breakfast. And for offering me a place to live. I promise not to be a burden."

She puts the car in reverse. As she's pulling away from the

curb, Daniel calls out, "Don't forget to text me when you leave work."

On the drive out to Foxtail, Casey's stomach knots as she rehearses her pitch to Ollie. What's the worst that can happen? Ollie can fire her, but she's quitting anyway. Or is she? After the things Daniel said in the park, Casey is not sure she can walk away from him now. She just needs a little more time to figure everything out.

CHAPTER 12

Ollie is seated at her desk in the office at Foxtail when Casey arrives. She broaches the subject of working remotely. She expects her request will upset her boss. But she's not prepared for the nuclear meltdown that occurs.

Ollie turns away from her computer and springs to her feet. "You're moving in with Daniel Love? Are you out of your mind?"

"It's only temporary. If you'll listen, I can explain."

"No way will I allow you to work on my marketing campaign in enemy territory. Daniel Love is undoubtedly bugging your room as we speak, planting video cameras in discreet locations to allow for unobstructed views of your laptop."

Casey holds back her temper. "You're wrong about Daniel. He doesn't run his business anymore. His children are in control."

"Just as I suspected. You've become one of them." Ollie holds out her hand, palm up. "Give me the graphics. I'll finish the marketing campaign myself."

Casey levels her gaze on Ollie. "Are you firing me?"

Ollie shrugs. "You're gonna quit anyway."

"On what grounds? Because I'm related to the Love family. That's discrimination, Ollie."

"Then sue me. I want you off my property immediately."

Ollie's face is red, and Casey worries she might explode. This woman is a hothead. She needs psychiatric help. The sooner Casey can get away from her, the better.

"Calm down, Ollie. If you'll give me a chance to explain, I have a solution that might work for both of us."

Ollie folds her arms over her chest. "You have three minutes. Start talking."

Casey drops her bag on the floor and sits on the edge of her desk. She explains about Ada's threats and the vandalism. "Daniel was kind enough to offer me a safe place to live. But I'm worried Ada will try to get to me here. Hence, the reason I asked to work remotely. Today is Thursday. If I stay focused and work through the weekend, I might finish the campaign by Monday."

"What happens after that? You're going to work for the Loves, aren't you?" Ollie palms her forehead. "I should've made you sign a non-compete clause."

"As of now, I have no plans to work at Love-Struck. Except for Sheldon, the Love children hate me. I'm their father's bastard child. Even if I were to one day work for Love-Struck, I would never divulge your business models."

Ollie is back on her feet. "Fine. Work remotely from Daniel's. But I'm counting on you to finish the campaign by Monday." She points at Casey's laptop on the desk. "Whatever you do, don't take your eyes off that computer. Sleep with it, if you have to," she says, and storms out of the office, slamming the door behind her.

Casey falls into her chair, taking a moment to collect herself before diving into her work. She doesn't come up for air until her stomach rumbles around noon.

Casey texts Fiona, asking if she can take a break for lunch.

Fiona responds right away. *Sure! Come on down. I'll grab a table for us.*

Casey is pleased to see business booming at the cafe. "This place is really hopping," she says when she joins Fiona at a table on the terrace.

Fiona beams. "Yes, it is. And I'm over the moon. Word is spreading about The Foxhole. I think we're on our way to success. Speaking of business, I don't have much time, so I asked one of the servers to bring us the salmon salad special. It's to die for, if I say so myself."

"I'm sure it is. We can talk another time if you need to get back to the kitchen."

"Not at all. Rumor has it you and Ollie had a fight." Fiona plants her elbows on the table, leaning in closer. "I'm dying to know about what."

"Word sure travels fast around here. Who told you?"

"A grounds crew member was weeding the flower bed outside the office window and overheard you all shouting."

"That's just great," Casey says, throwing up her hands. "Now the staff is gossiping about me. I can't catch a break."

The server arrives with their salads, and while they eat, Casey fills Fiona in on recent developments.

"When are you moving out?" Fiona asks, toying with her salad.

"This afternoon, after work." When Fiona's eyes fill with tears, Casey adds, "I'm sorry, Fi. With Ada on the loose, having me as a roommate is a safety hazard for you."

Fiona composes herself. "It's probably for the best. I have strong feelings for you, and living together only makes it that much harder. With you gone, hopefully I can clear my head."

"You have your blind date this weekend to look forward to."

"I know. And I'm excited. Will's taking me tubing on the Cowpasture river."

Casey grins. "I predict you and Will will hit it off, and your crush on me will be a dim memory, a fleeting moment of uncertainty about your sexuality."

"I hope you're right. I'm going to miss you, Casey. If you decide to leave town, I'll throw you a going away party."

Casey snorts out a laugh. "That'll be a small party. You, me, Daniel, and Sheldon. Everyone else in this town hates me."

"Jamie doesn't hate you."

"Maybe not. But his allegiance is to Ollie."

Fiona shakes her head, as though bewildered. "I don't understand why he lets her walk all over him."

"It's difficult to watch. Someone needs to clue him in before he makes a fool of himself. And that someone might be me, if I can summon the nerve."

Casey gets her opportunity after lunch when she runs into Jamie on her way back to the house.

"What'd you do to Ollie?" Jamie asks in an accusatory tone.

"It's a long story. But everything seems to set her off these days. You're a good guy, Jamie. You deserve better than the way she treats you."

Jamie lets out a humph. "You don't know what you're talking about. Ollie treats me just fine. She's the bomb. And I'm lucky to be with her."

"She's a bomb, all right. A ticking time bomb. And when she detonates, you'll be blown to smithereens in the explosion."

CHAPTER 13

Casey watches the sun sink below the horizon from the window of her appointed room at The Nest. She could get used to this life. A stunning view of the mountains from her corner suite. Walk-in closet offering shelves, cubbies, and drawers for her to store her clothes. Spacious marble bath featuring a spa tub and glass-enclosed shower with rain shower-head. Table on the terrace below, set for dinner with linens and candles.

Casey reminds herself her stay here is temporary, but the more time she spends with Daniel, the less inclined she is to leave Lovely. He's the main attraction. His concern for her well-being and safety have touched her deeply. He's a tender soul, a gentle lion. But his reputation as a shrewd businessman precedes him. She's certain that, when provoked, the lion will roar.

When she sees Daniel exit the house onto the terrace, she turns her back on the window and goes downstairs to join him.

He greets her with a peck on the cheek. "You look refreshed. Are you finding the accommodations suitable?"

"Like a five-star luxury resort. I've already unpacked and set up my desk in the study. I don't know how to thank you for all you've done for me."

"Allowing me to share your life is all the thanks I need. Marabella will be here momentarily with our first course. Shall we?" Daniel holds his hand out, and she walks ahead of him to the table. He pulls her chair out and waits until she's settled before taking his seat.

He uncorks a bottle of Viognier from another Virginia vineyard. She finds it odd he's not serving his own wine. Is he embarrassed by their product?

An attractive woman with caramel skin and hazel eyes appears on the terrace with a tray bearing two soup bowls. "Marabella, I'd like you to meet my daughter, Casey," Daniel says.

Casey's heart skips a beat. Hearing him call her his daughter legitimizes their relationship. "It's nice to meet you, Marabella."

She offers a shy smile in return. "Likewise."

"Marabella has worked for our family for decades. She does all the shopping and cooking. If you're craving anything special, she's your go-to gal."

"I don't wanna be any trouble."

"I consider it my pleasure," Marabella says. "I keep a grocery list on a notepad on the kitchen counter. Feel free to add anything you'd like or need. I shop for groceries on Mondays and Thursdays and at the farmers' market on Saturdays." She offers a slight bow before making her retreat.

"I have yet to find someone to replace Beatrice," Daniel says, his eyes on Marabella as she disappears inside the house. "The maid service comes every weekday. If you need anything, fresh towels or whatever, ask one of them."

"I can fend for myself. But thanks."

Daniel sinks his spoon into his cucumber gazpacho. "So . . . how did Ollie react when you asked to work remotely?"

"She was furious. She's convinced you're going to spy on me." Casey rolls her eyes. "As if you give a rat's ass about her marketing campaign. But she gave in when I promised to finish the project by Monday."

"So soon? Can you make that happen?"

"I'm going to do my best," Casey says with an enthusiasm she doesn't feel.

"It seems unfair of her to punish you because of your association with me. Tell me, why is she so upset with our family?"

Casey takes another bite of soup and wipes her lips with her napkin. "In a nutshell, Hugh and Charles are trying to force Ollie into selling Foxtail Farm to them. They sabotaged the renovations on her lodge, including damaging the countertop for her tasting bar. I don't have details. Most of that happened before I came. The contractor reported everything to the sheriff. He could probably tell you more. I know for a fact, they called animal control on Ollie's dogs. It's partially her fault for not controlling them."

"They want the land to build their golf resort, a project I never approved of," Daniel says and grows pensive while Casey finishes her gazpacho.

Marabella serves the main course—seared scallops accompanied by slices of cheesy tomato pie and broccolini—and clears away the soup bowls.

Casey samples the tomato pie. "What an unusual combination of flavors."

"One of my favorite dishes. There's nothing better than summer-ripe tomatoes." Daniel takes a bite and moans in pleasure. "I'm sorry you got caught in the middle between Ollie and my boys. But not everyone is against you. I've got your back. I promise everything will work out."

That's a promise she's not sure Daniel can keep. Casey is caught in the middle, not only between Ollie and the Loves but among the Love children themselves. She suspects Daniel underestimates his offspring. Sheldon is on Casey's side, but the rest of them wish her dead.

Casey is working in her study midmorning on Friday when she hears loud voices coming from downstairs. Cracking open the door, she makes certain the coast is clear before tiptoeing across the hall to the window in the guest room opposite hers. Parked haphazardly in the driveway below are Ada's Mercedes, Sheldon's Range Rover, a silver Tahoe, and a gray Silverado pickup truck. Returning to the hall, she creeps toward the stairs and crouches down behind a chest of drawers.

"You can't do that!" Ada shrills from the living room at the base of the stairs.

"I can, and I am," Daniel says in a steady tone. "As of this minute, I'm taking back control of Love-Struck Vineyards."

Casey's hand flies to her mouth to stifle a gasp. The lion is roaring.

"But we all own shares in the company," says Hugh or Charles. Casey doesn't know them well enough to decipher their voices. "We have to vote you back in."

Daniel coughs, clearing his throat. "Collectively, the four of you own twenty-four percent of the business. I own the other seventy-six percent. I can do anything I damn well please. And Love-Struck Vineyards is long overdue a reset."

Loud and angry murmurs fill the house.

A finger whistle silences the group.

"You have only yourselves to blame," Daniel says. "Three years ago, when I turned the vineyard over to you to manage, I gave you a set of guidelines to follow, which you have ignored. And I established goals for the business, which you have not achieved. Instead, you've wasted valuable time and money chasing your silly dream of building a golf resort after I made it clear I will never support that project."

"But, Dad, we stand to make billions. If only we can get our hands on Foxtail Farm." Casey assumes this is Hugh, the ring-leader in the charge to buy Ollie out.

"I'm well aware of your bullying campaign to get rid of Ollie," Daniel says. "And I don't approve of your tactics. I will not tolerate unethical behavior."

"This is all because of her!" Ada cries. "Your little bastard daughter!"

"Shh! Lower your voice. She's upstairs working," Daniel says.

"What's she doing working in *our* house?" Ada yells.

"It's Dad's house. And Casey is living here now." Even though Casey can't see him, Sheldon's amused tone tells her how delighted he is to deliver this blow.

There's a loud thud, as though someone stomped their foot, and Ada says, "Ugh! I don't believe this."

"Believe it," Daniel says. "Casey is now part of my life. And starting tomorrow, I'm back at work full-time. You can either work with me, or you can find employment elsewhere."

Thundering footsteps, like a herd of elephants tromping on the hardwood floors, are followed by the slamming of the front door.

Casey hears laughter. "Dad! You were brilliant," Sheldon says. "They deserved that. Heck, I deserve it. I've been complacent in letting them do whatever they want. Welcome back."

"Thank you, son. Unfortunately, I'm afraid we're in for a rough road ahead."

A feeling of impending doom overcomes Casey as she sneaks back to her study. She hopes Daniel knows what he's doing. Because Hugh, Charles, and Ada will never accept her now.

Casey receives a text from Daniel around three o'clock. *Can you take a break from work? I need to talk to you about something.*

She thumbs off her response. *Sure. Give me a few.*

I'll meet you on the terrace. Daniel texts back.

Casey freshens her face and pulls on a clean white T-shirt over her jeans before heading downstairs.

Daniel is waiting for her on the terrace. "Let's go for a walk around the grounds."

She follows him out the back door, across the terrace, and down the hill. Instead of going to the rose garden, he takes a dirt path to an old wooden bridge that crosses a gently flowing stream.

"Are there fish in this stream?" Casey asks, peering over the side of the bridge.

"Biggest mountain trout you've ever seen," Daniel says proudly. "There are many hidden gems on this property. I hope you'll have the opportunity to explore them."

"I hope so too." Even if she moves away, she can still come back for long visits.

"I trust you heard the commotion earlier," Daniel says.

Casey experiences a pang of guilt for eavesdropping. "I heard voices. I thought they were coming from outside."

"I notified my children that I was reclaiming my place as head of Love-Struck. They are furious. Well, three of them anyway. Sheldon supports me."

Casey turns her back to the stream and props herself against the railing. "I hope this isn't because of me."

"Truth be told, I should never have given them control. I had in mind to travel the world, visit all the best fly-fishing destinations. I tried it. But traveling alone doesn't have much appeal." Daniel takes a sip of his drink. "I've been restless lately. I didn't realize how bored I was until today. It felt good to exercise my influence again. Lord knows, I have my work cut out for me, righting my children's wrongs. I'd like to start by apologizing to Ollie. Do you think she would meet with me?"

Casey stares down at her tennis shoes. "Gosh, Daniel. I don't know. Ollie lost her parents a couple of years ago. She's volatile right now. Every time I predict she'll do one thing, she does the exact opposite."

"I'm sorry to hear about her parents. That makes me more determined than ever to make amends." Placing a hand at the small of her back, Daniel guides Casey off the other side of the bridge toward a field of wildflowers. "Perhaps you and Ollie can work out your differences. She'd be a fool to let you go. You're extremely talented. Your designs are eye-catching."

The hairs on her neck stand up. "Where have you seen my designs?"

Daniel chuckles. "I haven't been spying on you, if that's what you're thinking. The new brands for The Foxhole and Foxtail Farm are all over the Internet."

Casey relaxes. "Oh. Right. Thanks."

Daniel picks a small bouquet and hands them to her. When they turn and start back toward the house, he asks, "Would you ever consider a job at Love-Struck? We currently employ an outside advertising agency. But their recent work has been uninspiring. We need someone with a fresh vision like you."

"I don't think that's a good idea, considering how your children feel about me. I value my life."

"And I can protect you," he says with a mischievous smile.

"By keeping me locked up like a jailbird?" She nudges him with her elbow. "Never mind the birdie's nest is seriously cool."

"I have no intention of keeping my beautiful new daughter hidden away from the world." Daniel kisses her cheek. "Just think about my offer. I have the upper hand. My kids will either go along with the reorganization or they can find work elsewhere."

Reorganization? Earlier, when talking to Sheldon in the living room, Daniel had used the word *reset*. Reset implies starting over anew. Reorganization means a restructuring of the company. Whatever the lion has in mind, Casey is not sure she wants to be around to witness the attack.

CHAPTER 14

Casey ventures downstairs at dinnertime on Friday, hoping to spend some more time with Daniel. She discovers a note from Marabella on the kitchen counter, explaining that Daniel had dinner plans and that she left a bowl of Thai chicken salad for Casey in the refrigerator.

Dinner plans? With whom? Is he seeing someone? Funny, he mentioned nothing during their walk earlier.

Casey makes herself a plate and returns to her study, where she remains until past midnight, listening with one ear for the sound of Daniel's footfalls on the stairs. When she turns in around one, he still hasn't come home. And when she wakes early the following morning, Daniel's SUV is missing from the driveway.

Casey trods down the back stairs to the kitchen where she finds a tray of Danishes on the counter but no sign of Marabella. Then she remembers the cook goes to the farmers' market on Saturdays. She makes coffee, grabs a banana muffin, and retreats to her suite.

She works through lunch and is finalizing schedules for the advertising campaign midafternoon when Sheldon bursts into her study.

Heart pounding in chest, she spins around in her chair. "You scared me. Did you ever hear of knocking?"

"My family has an open-door policy. Get up. You're coming with me." Grabbing her hand, he hauls her out of the chair. "You need to take a break to clear your head."

He drags her down the stairs, and when they reach the center hallway, she latches onto the living room door casing. "Stop! Sheldon! Where are you taking me?"

"It's a surprise." He pries her fingers loose, tosses her over his shoulder, and carries her out to his Range Rover. He deposits her in the passenger seat and runs around to the driver's side.

"Seriously, Sheldon. I'm on a deadline. Every minute counts."

"We won't be gone long," he says, and speeds off down the driveway.

Casey hastily fastens her seat belt. "Will you at least tell me where you're taking me?"

He glances over at her. "To Connie's Cones for ice cream."

Her jaw slackens. "I was on a roll, and you're interrupting my mojo for *ice cream*?"

"Not just any ice cream. Connie's is the best in Virginia. Besides, we need to talk."

Casey presses her head against the window. "I figured. About what? Did something happen?"

"I'll tell you when we get there."

Connie's is an Aerostream trailer converted into a food truck. A wooden deck offers seating at umbrellaed tables, which are currently all occupied.

"You go ahead," Casey says when he parks the car. "I'm not much for ice cream."

"I'll be right back." Leaving the car running, he returns a minute later with two towering cones of ice cream.

"I told you I don't want any," Casey says with a huff of irritation.

"It's salted caramel. You have to at least taste it," he says, thrusting the cone at her.

With one hand on the steering wheel, Sheldon maneuvers the car out of the parking lot and away from town.

"Where are we going now?" She examines the ice cream, the smell making her stomach rumble.

"Just up the road a bit. You'll see."

Remembering she hasn't eaten since breakfast, Casey takes a tentative lick. The texture is creamy and the combination of salt and sweet rich. "Okay, this is seriously good," she says, sinking her teeth into the ice cream.

"I told you," Sheldon says, dragging his tongue up the ice cream cone.

They drive about a mile before Sheldon pulls off the road at an overlook offering an impressive view of Love-Struck Vineyards. They get out of the Range Rover and sit down at a picnic table. "Okay, spill it. What did you want to talk to me about?" Casey asks.

Sheldon reaches across the table for her free hand, giving it a squeeze. "First, let me just say what a welcomed addition you are to the family. I'm thrilled to have a sane sibling I can talk to about family matters."

"Let's hope I can stay sane," Casey says, under her breath.

"You will. Because you have me. And Dad."

"Thank you. That means a lot, Sheldon." She wipes her lips with a napkin.

"You should be aware our siblings are up to something. They haven't been into the office since Dad announced his reset or reorganization or whatever it is. Their cars were parked at Hugh's house all afternoon yesterday."

"What do you think they're scheming?"

"A way to get rid of Dad. And you. Maybe even me."

Her appetite suddenly gone, Casey walks her cone over to the trash can. "What exactly is your role within the company?" she asks, returning to the table.

"I'm the overseer," he says, and she laughs. "That sounds like a cush job."

"That's the way Hugh intended it. His goal was to get me out of the way and make me dispensable. I've fooled them into thinking I don't do anything. But I know every staff member personally, and I can work every piece of machinery. I'm more aware of our company's strengths and weaknesses than the three of them put together. My siblings have their individual responsibilities. Ada manages the tasting room and event planning. Hugh runs the winery and oversees wine production. And Charles oversees the vineyard. If necessary, I could run the whole kit and caboodle. I knew this day would come. And I planned for it." Sheldon balls up his napkin and tosses it at the trash can, cheering when it goes in.

"This day being?"

"The day Dad gets fed up with their shenanigans and comes back to work."

They stand together and walk back toward the car. "You, Casey,"—he gives her ponytail a yank—"are the catalyst that facilitated Dad's sudden renewed interest in the business."

Casey is flattered to think she had such a profound impact on her father. "You're giving me too much credit. I don't think his renewed interest is all that sudden. Daniel, himself, told me he's bored with the life of leisure."

"That may be so, but you're the one who inspired him to make a move."

Casey opens her car door, but she doesn't get in. "I hope I didn't get you in trouble, Sheldon. I informed Daniel that Hugh and Charles have been harassing Ollie."

Sheldon collapses against the car. "I'm aware. And I'm not gonna lie, Dad was pretty pissed at me about that. Bottom line, I shouldn't have kept it from him."

Casey leans against the door. "Why did you? You were adamant I tell him about Ada. I got the impression you didn't keep secrets from him."

"That was different. I was concerned for your safety. When it comes to my brothers, I prefer to let them dig their own graves.

Besides, I was trying to handle the situation. And I failed. I still have a lot to learn."

Casey pouts her lower lip. "I'm sorry, Sheldon."

Sheldon chucks her chin. "Don't sweat it, Casey. It's not all bad. Dad and I had a long overdue heart-to-heart discussion about a number of things."

"I'm glad to hear it," Casey says, sliding onto the passenger seat.

Sheldon closes her door and goes around the car to the driver's side.

As they head off toward town, Casey asks, "Does Daniel have a girlfriend?"

"Not that I know of. Why do you ask?"

"He went out to dinner last night and never came home. His Audi wasn't in the driveway this morning."

"Go, Dad," Sheldon says with a naughty twinkle in his olive eyes. "Whoever she is, I'm happy for him. I worry about him being lonely."

Casey wonders what other secrets Daniel is keeping.

They pull up in front of The Nest, and Casey opens the door to get out. "Thanks for the ice cream. And the warning. Should I be worried about my safety?"

"Just be on alert. We grew up here. The Nest is our home. We all have keys, and we usually come and go at will."

An uneasy feeling sours Casey's stomach as she makes her way to the house. She stops by the kitchen for a glass of ice water before climbing the back staircase to her suite of rooms. Instead of passing through her bedroom, she enters her study from the hallway where she finds Ada, dressed in black with a black baseball cap pulled low over her head, rifling through her drawings.

"What do you think you're doing?" Casey asks.

A startled Ada spins around, gripping the drawings to her chest. "Trying to figure out what you're up to."

Casey strides across the room and snatches the drawings from her. "Give me those before you wrinkle them. If you'd asked, I would've told you I'm working on a project for Foxtail. Not that it's any of your business." She gathers up the papers strewn across her desk and stuffs them into a file folder.

"You're a perfect stranger living in my father's house, which makes it my business."

Casey turns around, shielding her desk with her body. "I'm a guest here. Daniel invited me to stay as long as I like."

Ada lets out a humph. "You may have weaseled your way into his life, but you'll never get your hands on our family's business."

"News flash, Ada! I'm not interested in your family's business."

"I don't believe you." Ada plucks a lock of Casey's hair free of its ponytail. "I don't know what Daddy sees in you anyway." Fingering the curl, she says, "What color is this? If you're going for blonde, you missed the mark. It's brassy at best."

Casey slaps Ada's hand away.

Ada's upper lip curls as she scrutinizes Casey's features. "You're pretty enough at first glance. But your forehead is too broad and your eyes too wide. Daddy's infatuation with you won't last. He'll eventually tire of you. And when he does, you'll be out on your backside."

Something inside of Casey snaps. She's had enough of this spiteful cow. "You're wrong, Ada. I'm a breath of fresh air compared to you. Daniel is fed up with your nasty attitude and unethical business practices. He's kicking *you* out on *your* butt. Isn't that what this *reorganization* is about? He'll throw you out of the company first and then out of his life."

An angry flush mottles Ada's skin, creeping up her neck to her cheeks. "We'll see about that," she snarls, and storms out of the study.

Following her into the hall, Casey calls after her, "For your information, my hair color is natural, the same golden hue as Sheldon's."

Retreating to her study, she locks the door behind her and hurries to the window, watching Ada flee on foot down the hill toward the winery. The Love siblings set Casey up. Sheldon lured her away on a surprise outing while Ada broke into her office. Although technically, it wasn't a break in because Casey left the door wide open.

Ollie's words come back to Casey as she sits down at her desk to assess the damage. *Whatever you do, don't take your eyes off that computer. Sleep with it if you have to.* Yet Casey left it unattended in the middle of enemy territory. Her computer is password protected, but copies of the nearly completed marketing campaign —graphics and budgets, lists of vendors and schedules—are neatly organized in files on top of her desk.

Casey falls back in her chair. There's nothing top secret in the documents. Casey's graphics are original to Foxtail. And all marketers use the same social media outlets. So what if Ada knows how much money Foxtail is planning to spend on advertising? There's no way she can use that against them.

Eager to complete this project, Casey sits up straight, opens her computer, and gets back to work.

CHAPTER 15

E arly evening on Saturday, Casey is typing up the marketing schedule on her computer when someone taps lightly on the door. Her heart skips a beat, and she turns toward the door. "Who is it?" she calls out in a tentative voice.

"It's Marabella, Miss Casey. May I have a word with you before I leave for the day?"

"Of course." Casey scrambles to her feet and unlocks the door.

"I'm off on Sundays. There's a chicken tetrazzini casserole in the refrigerator for your dinner tonight, and I made shrimp salad and cut up a bowl of fresh fruit for your meals tomorrow."

"Thank you, Marabella. I didn't mean for you to go to so much trouble. Is my father home yet?" Casey feels like a fraud referring to Daniel as her father, but Marabella doesn't seem to mind.

Marabella casts her gaze downward. "No, ma'am. He won't be home until tomorrow. He's at a wedding in Charlottesville."

"A wedding? Your note said he had dinner plans last night. Why didn't you tell me he was out of town for the weekend?"

Marabella shrinks back at the sound of Casey's harsh tone. "I didn't know until he texted me this afternoon. Mr. Love rarely shares his plans with me."

Casey rests a reassuring hand on the cook's shoulder. "I'm sorry. I didn't mean to jump down your throat. I'm on edge trying to finish my project." She closes her study door. "I'll walk out with you. I'm going down anyway, to get a drink."

Relief washes over Marabella's face. "I just made a fresh pitcher of sweet tea."

"Iced tea sounds refreshing," Casey says, even though she has something stronger in mind.

In the kitchen, Marabella grabs her canvas tote bag off the counter and opens the back door. "I'll see you on Monday, then."

Forcing a smile, Casey locks the bolt and leans against the door. Monday sounds like a long way off. She's alone in this ginormous house with the possibility of Ada and Hugh lurking around. She'll be lucky if she catches a wink of sleep.

Casey pops the tetrazzini in the oven and opens a bottle of rosé, pouring herself a generous glass. After checking to make certain all the windows and doors are locked, she wanders about the vast rooms downstairs, inspecting Daniel's extensive art collection and admiring the exotic animals—trophies she assumes are from an African safari—adorning the walls in his wood-paneled study. On the ebony baby grand piano in the living room, she studies the framed photographs of the Love children taken throughout the years. Their mother is captured in many of the photographs. She's a striking woman, although she bears little resemblance to her daughter. Lila's hair is lighter, more caramel to Ada's rich expresso, and her eyes are deep blue. Who does Ada take after if not her mother or her father?

Feeling adventurous, Casey ascends the main staircase to the master suite. Daniel's bedroom is handsomely decorated with navy walls, lush cream carpeting, and bed linens in shades of khaki. His bathroom is much like Casey's, only larger, and a pair of french doors offer a more widespread view of the mountains than hers. Stepping out onto the small balcony, she stretches out on the wicker chaise lounge and sips the rest of her wine while watching the sun change the sky from orange to pink on its descent below the horizon.

When her glass is empty, Casey returns to the kitchen, scarfs down two healthy scoops of tetrazzini and takes the rest of the bottle of wine upstairs to her study. She works until the bottle is empty and her computer screen blurred. Making certain both doors are locked, she crawls beneath the luxurious comforter and turns on the wide-screen television. She clicks on the first season of *Emily in Paris* on Netflix and passes out midway through the first episode.

Casey is reading through her marketing materials one last time midafternoon on Sunday when someone taps on the door and tries to turn the knob. "Casey, it's me, Daniel. Are you in there?"

Casey swings open the door. She has in mind to rip him a new one for leaving her in this big house alone. But she loses her nerve when she sees his bewildered expression.

He gestures at the doorknob. "Why's the door locked?"

"I didn't realize you were home."

He waits for her to say more. When she doesn't, he shifts his weight to the other foot. "We're on our own for dinner. I've got a hankering for a cheeseburger. Care to join me?"

"Sure. But I haven't showered today. Can you give me a few minutes?"

"Of course. Take your time. I'll start getting everything ready." He hesitates as though he wants to say something and then turns back toward the stairs.

Casey spends longer than normal in the shower, letting the hot water massage her aching shoulders while she ponders how much to say to Daniel about what happened over the weekend. Ultimately, she decides it is best to tell him the truth about everything. Including her irritation over him leaving town without telling her.

Daniel is in the kitchen making hamburger patties when she comes down the backstairs. "Can I offer you a glass of wine?" He nods at the bottle of white wine on the counter, a vintage from another Virginia vineyard instead of his own.

Casey still has a dull headache from the wine she drank last night. "No, thanks. I'll just have some tea," she says, removing the pitcher from the refrigerator.

Daniel adds the platter of burgers to a tray already loaded with seasoning salt, metal spatula, and hamburger rolls. "All right then. Let's get this party started," he says, and they move out to the terrace.

Daniel coats the grates with cooking spray, and Casey transfers the burgers from the tray. Lowering the grill's lid, Daniel says, "I hate to press the issue, but I need to know why you had your door locked. Did you feel unsafe in the house alone?"

"I did, after I found Ada going through the files on my desk," Casey says, and explains about her ice cream excursion with Sheldon and subsequent encounter with Ada.

Daniel listens with face set in stone. "I told Alfred to have his team patrol the property every half hour."

Casey wrinkles her brow. "Who's Alfred?"

"The head of my private security detail."

"That's funny. I never saw a patrol car. Then again, I had no reason to be on the lookout for one. Maybe if you'd told me you were going away."

"I'm a grown man, Casey. My whereabouts are none of your concern."

Daniel's cross tone both intimidates and irritates Casey. She inhales a deep breath and forges on. "That may be so. But you invited me to stay here for safety reasons. After *your* daughter vandalized my car and home. You should've at least warned me I'd be alone in the house. You never even mentioned a trip when we walked on Friday afternoon. Bare minimum, you should have given me Alfred's number in case I needed to contact him."

"I'm not used to feeling obligated to anyone." Daniel takes his anger out on the burgers, flipping them over and over with the spatula.

Heat radiates through Casey's body. "Really? You're a father of four. You should let your loved ones know what's going on in your life. For safety's sake, if for no other reason. Mom and I always stayed in touch." She shrugs. "Then again, it was only the two of us, so what do I know about how large families operate?"

Daniel deflates. "When you put it that way, I guess I should've told you."

He takes the burgers off the grill, and they go inside to fix their plates. He waits until they're settled at the breakfast counter before continuing the conversation. "I wasn't at a wedding. I was supposed to go to Charlottesville, but at the last minute, I canceled and drove down to our house at Virginia Beach. I'm considering making some drastic changes at the vineyard. Getting away helped me put things into perspective and ponder the ramifications of my actions." He spreads Dijon mustard on his hamburger bun. "I'm sorry I didn't tell you where I was going. I apologize if you were frightened because of me."

"No worries. I worked most of the weekend anyway."

Daniel leans into her, nudging her with his arm. "You're wrong about one thing."

"What's that?" Casey asks and takes a bite of her burger.

"I'm a father of five now."

Casey's heart warms, and a smile spreads across her face. "Yes, you are."

He raises his wineglass. "Are you sure you won't have a splash? It'll help you sleep better."

"I'm positive. I want to have a clear head when I meet with Ollie in the morning."

"About that. I've tried reaching out to Ollie, but she hasn't responded. I was thinking I'd go with you to Foxtail in the morning. I only need a few minutes of Ollie's time."

Casey imagines Ollie's tantrum when she sees Daniel at her front door. "I'm not sure that's a good idea."

He waves away her concern. "It'll be fine. We'll drive two cars. When I'm done, you can proceed with your presentation."

His determined scowl tells her he's made up his mind. "It's not a presentation. I'm turning the marketing campaign over to Ollie to implement."

"What happens after that? Do you think she'll ask you to stay on?"

"I have no clue." Casey is tired of thinking about her future. She certainly doesn't want to talk about it tonight.

"Don't commit to anything until you and I talk. I'm not ready to discuss details yet. But I may have a proposition for you."

CHAPTER 16

Casey is too weary to press Daniel about his proposition at dinner. But when she gets into bed two hours later, her imagination wanders. The potential what-ifs make her head spin. What if Ollie is blown away by the marketing campaign and begs her to stay on at Foxtail? What if Daniel offers her a position at Love-Struck?

Casey always intended her job at Foxtail to be temporary, a way to earn a living until she met her father. And she finds it difficult to envision herself working at Love-Struck. Her half siblings would resent her more than they already do. The third option is to look for a job in a different town. Like Charlotte and Nashville, Richmond is an up-and-coming Southern city, and it's only two hours away. She could visit Daniel for holidays and long weekends.

When Casey finally falls asleep around midnight, she's all but decided to start a new life with a clean slate in Richmond.

A storm system blows in overnight, and rain is pouring down in torrents as she drives over to Foxtail at eight on Monday morning. A wave of nausea engulfs her as she spots Daniel's headlights in her rearview mirror. She has a bad feeling about this.

Ollie is on the porch with a cup of coffee and her iPad when they arrive. Hearing their footsteps, she smiles up from her iPad, as though expecting to see Casey. And then she frowns at the sight of Daniel standing next to Casey in the doorway. "What're you doing here?"

Daniel steps onto the porch. "You won't return my phone calls, so I thought I'd come in person. I only need a minute of your time."

Casey closes the french doors behind him to give them privacy. While they talk, she pours a cup of coffee and organizes her files on the counter. Daniel is on the porch for less than five minutes. When he passes through the kitchen on his way out, he winks at Casey, signaling that his meeting went as expected.

When Ollie enters the kitchen, Casey asks, "Is everything okay?"

Ollie shrugs. "He apologized and promised things would be better from now on. We'll see if he delivers."

Casey sweeps an arm at the documents covering the counter. "I'm ready if you are."

For the next ninety minutes, they go over the marketing campaign in extensive detail. Although Ollie asks knowledgeable questions, Casey gets the impression she's overwhelmed at the prospect of managing the marketing.

"Excellent work." Ollie gathers the documents in a neat stack on the counter. "I'd like for you to continue working here, Casey. At least for another month on a trial basis. We hit a rough patch, but I'm sure we can get back on track."

"You and I both know this won't work," Casey says, the words rolling off her tongue without hesitation or remorse. "Your new branding is in place. The marketing campaign is set to launch. You don't need a graphics designer going forward. You should hire an assistant to help you with the administrative stuff."

"Is there anything I can do to change your mind?"

Casey shakes her head. "I'm sorry. This is for the best."

"What will you do?"

"I'm not sure yet. I may look for a job in Richmond. For now, I'm going to take a few days off to rest. I've been working all weekend on the campaign, and I'm tired." Casey closes the laptop and slips off the barstool. "Goodbye, Ollie. I wish you the best of luck with the vineyard."

"Goodbye, Casey. Text me your address, and I'll mail you your last paycheck."

Leaving the laptop on the counter, Casey exits the house feeling pounds lighter. She enjoyed the work at Foxtail, but she's relieved to be rid of Ollie's negative vibes.

The rain has moved out, but the sky is still gray. She returns to her room at The Nest and crawls, fully clothed, into bed. She falls into a deep slumber and is awakened hours later by a house-keeper who introduces herself as Henrietta, Beatrice's replacement.

"Mr. Love wants you to join him in the dining room for lunch at noon."

Casey glances at the alarm clock on the nightstand. "But that's in ten minutes."

"Yes'm. He's expecting guests and asked for you to please dress accordingly."

So much for the relaxing afternoon she'd planned. "Thanks, Henrietta. Tell him I'll be right down."

Casey rolls out of bed and smooths the wrinkles out of her gray work dress. Dragging herself to the bathroom, she splashes cold water on her face and fastens her hair in a tight knot at her nape. She smears a pale lipstick across her lips, rubs her lips together, and smiles at her reflection in the mirror. Game on.

Casey hears loud voices as she descends the main staircase, but the dining room goes silent when she appears in the doorway. Her eyes travel the table. As Casey suspected, the Love children are the guests Henrietta mentioned.

At the far end of the room, Daniel gets up from the head of the table to greet her. Sheldon follows suit, but the older Love brothers remain seated.

"Casey, so good of you to join us." Daniel pulls out the chair to his right, which Casey knows from her mother's elegant dinner parties is the place of honor.

Head high and shoulders back, Casey walks toward him and sits down next to Sheldon. No one speaks while the waitstaff bustles about, filling flutes of champagne and serving plates loaded with wedges of quiche, mixed green salad, and buttery yeast rolls.

When the servers have departed the room, Daniel bows his head and offers a prayer. "Amen." He raises his glass. "To new beginnings."

The rest of the table mumbles, "To new beginnings."

Daniel lifts his fork and begins eating.

Ada downs the champagne and sets the glass on the table. "What's this about, Daddy?"

Casey risks a glance across the table at Ada. She's seated between Hugh and the brother Casey assumes is Charles, although they have yet to be introduced. Ada's lips are pursed tight as she glares at Casey through angry eyes.

"I'll explain over dessert," Daniel says.

Ada consults her Apple Watch. "Let's talk while we eat. I have a meeting at one."

Irritation crosses Daniel's face. He doesn't like to be told what to do. "Have it your way. I called this meaning to announce my restructuring plans for the company. I'll be redistributing some shares. I'll keep fifty-one percent, but I'm giving Casey and Sheldon twenty-five percent. You, Charles, and Hugh will share twenty-four."

When the table erupts in angry protests, Daniel taps his knife on his glass. "Just hear me out."

Ignoring him, Hugh blurts, "You're giving Sheldon more control. What's in it for us?"

"You get to keep your jobs," Daniel explains. "Or some variation of them."

An awkward silence settles over the room as Ada exchanges nervous glances with Hugh and Charles. Sheldon wears a satisfied smirk, like the cat who swallowed the canary.

Daniel returns to eating. "I'm bringing Casey onboard to establish a marketing department. Her job will be to create a fresh new brand as she's done at Foxtail. I expect you all to provide your input, but ultimately she'll have full creative control."

Daniel turns his attention to his oldest sons. "Hugh, you and Charles will spend the next few months in the fields, learning the business of growing grapes. In the meantime, I'll be interviewing winemakers. At the end of harvest, we will start the process of improving our product." He points at each of them in turn. "But before you do anything, you will go next door and apologize to Ollie for the trouble you've caused her."

"Absolutely not." Hugh tosses his napkin on his plate and pushes back from the table. "I'm wearing Ollie down. She's starting to cave. And I want that property for our resort."

Daniel's face glows red. "I'm officially canceling the plans for the resort. And I don't mean temporarily."

Hugh jumps up, nearly knocking his chair over. "Then Charles and I are outta here," he says, bopping Charles on the head.

Charles looks down at his plate, but he doesn't budge.

"Suit yourself," Hugh says to Charles. "You won't last one day as a farmer."

Hugh strides across the room. When he reaches the doorway, Daniel says in a commanding voice, "If you leave this house, you'll never be welcome here again."

Hugh stops in his tracks and returns to his seat without further argument.

"Will my job change?" Ada asks, the demanding tone of voice from earlier noticeably gone.

"You're in charge of event planning."

Ada scoffs, "But what about tasting room?"

"Sheldon will manage the winery and tasting room. Among other things."

Ada appears as though she might cry. "What other things?"

"Sheldon will be my right-hand man for the foreseeable future. My goal is for the five of you to learn to work together for the betterment of the company. In two years' time, if we've accomplished my objectives, I'll consider turning most of the company over to you to manage as a team."

Casey smiles to herself as she listens to Ada, Hugh, and Charles plead with their father to change his mind about the reorganization. But Casey knows he won't. His plan is genius, a way to accomplish his objectives, determine which of his children are loyal, and separate the wheat from the chaff.

"I'm willing to go along with your little scheme on one condition," Ada says, wagging her pointer finger at her father.

Daniel stares down his nose at her. "What condition, Ada?"

"I want Goldilocks to take a DNA test." Ada trains her finger gun at Casey and pretends to fire.

Casey gives a nonchalant shrug. "I'm fine with that. I have nothing to hide."

Daniel smirks in triumph. "I anticipated this request. In the spirit of team building, we should all have DNA tests. Where we go one, we go all. I hired a private nurse. She's waiting in the living room to collect your sample."

Ada stands abruptly. "Excuse me, but I've lost my appetite. And I have to get to my meeting."

When Hugh and Charles get up to follow her, Daniel calls out, "Don't forget to deposit your DNA on your way out."

Casey bites on her lip to keep from laughing.

Once the others have gone, Daniel turns to Casey. "What do you think? Will you stay?"

Casey grins. No way will she pass up this chance. "Yes, sir. Thank you for the opportunity. I won't let you down."

Daniel beams. "I knew we could count on you."

"There's one thing I need to clear the air about." Her gaze bounces from Daniel to Sheldon. "On Saturday, when I returned from our ice cream outing, I found Ada in my study, going through my files. Did you know about that?"

"Not until Dad told me about it this morning," Sheldon says without hesitation. "Our professional relationship won't work unless we all trust one another. I promised Dad I won't keep secrets from him. We need to know we can count on you to do the same."

These two new men in her life may be flawed, but Casey's intuition tells her they have her best interests at heart. "You can trust me. I promise not to keep secrets."

"It's always been Dad and me against them," Sheldon says. "We were two and now we're three."

Daniel lifts his glass. "To us."

Sheldon follows suit. "Welcome to the fam, Casey."

As she clinks their glasses, an excitement like she's never experienced before flitters across her chest. Her life just got a heck of a lot more interesting.

Are you dying to know the results of the DNA tests? You may be surprised, but you won't be disappointed. Family drama and romantic suspense continue with Casey, Ollie, and Ada in the next installment of the series, *Blind Love*. Preorder your copy now. Click HERE for links.

If you're loving the Virginia Vineyard series, you might enjoy my Palmetto Island and Hope Springs series as well. Watch the trailers and learn more on my website.

. . .

And . . . to find out about my new and upcoming books, be sure to sign up for my newsletter.

Be sure to visit my website where you'll find a host of information regarding my inspiration for writing as well as book trailers, reviews, and Pinterest boards from my 20+ other books.

ALSO BY ASHLEY FARLEY

Virginia Vineyards

Love Child

Blind Love

Palmetto Island

Muddy Bottom

Change of Tides

Lowcountry on My Mind

Sail Away

Hope Springs Series

Dream Big, Stella!

Show Me the Way

Mistletoe and Wedding Bells

Matters of the Heart

Road to New Beginnings

Stand Alone

On My Terms

Tangled in Ivy

Lies that Bind

Life on Loan

Only One Life

Home for Wounded Hearts

Nell and Lady

Sweet Tea Tuesdays

Saving Ben

ABOUT THE AUTHOR

Ashley Farley writes books about women for women. Her characters are mothers, daughters, sisters, and wives facing real-life issues. Her bestselling Sweeney Sisters series has touched the lives of many.

Ashley is a wife and mother of two young adult children. While she's lived in Richmond, Virginia, for the past twenty-one years, a piece of her heart remains in the salty marshes of the South Carolina Lowcountry, where she still calls home. Through the eyes of her characters, she captures the moss-draped trees, delectable cuisine, and kindhearted folk with lazy drawls that make the area so unique.

Ashley loves to hear from her readers. Visit Ashley's website @ ashleyfarley.com

Get free exclusive content by signing up for her newsletter @ ashleyfarley.com/newsletter-signup/